LEAP INTO DANGER!

Joe watched the pole vaulter approach the box. His sprinting and planting form were perfect. With a mighty heave, Chuck launched himself upward. As the pole started its snap-back, he swung his legs up, using all the force to send himself over the crossbar. It looked like a faultless vault.

Then Joe heard a sickening sound—a brittle snap.

Instinctively Joe rushed toward the pit. But by the time he got there, he realized he was helpless.

Chuck's pole had snapped in two, leaving the star vaulter upside down and unsupported fifteen feet above the ground.

Books in THE HARDY BOYS CASEFILES™ Series

Available from ARCHWAY Paperbacks

THE HARDY BOYS

CASEFILES™

NO. 111

COMPETITIVE EDGE

FRANKLIN W. DIXON

AN ARCHWAY PAPERBACK
Published by POCKET BOOKS
New York London Toronto Sydney Tokyo Singapore

Ingram 4/12/96 #3⁹⁹

AN ARCHWAY PAPERBACK *Original*

An Archway Paperback published by
POCKET BOOKS, a division of Simon & Schuster Inc.
1230 Avenue of the Americas, New York, NY 10020

Copyright © 1996 by Simon & Schuster Inc.
Produced by Mega-Books, Inc.

ISBN: 0-671-50446-0

First Archway Paperback printing May 1996

10 9 8 7 6 5 4 3 2 1

THE HARDY BOYS, AN ARCHWAY PAPERBACK and colophon are registered trademarks of Simon & Schuster Inc.

THE HARDY BOYS CASEFILES is a trademark of Simon & Schuster Inc.

Cover photograph from "The Hardy Boys" Series © 1995 Nelvana Limited/Marathon Productions S.A. All Rights Reserved.

Logo Design ™ & © 1995 by Nelvana Limited. All Rights Reserved.

Printed in the U.S.A.

IL 6+

Chapter

1

"THIS IS AN OUTRAGE!" the huge man yelled, pounding the registration desk at the Olympic Village residence hall. "How can you put me in the same building with these traitors? They should not even be allowed to participate in the games."

Joe Hardy watched the registration clerk try to calm the man down, but whatever she said just seemed to enrage the athlete more.

Milling around Joe in the lobby were hundreds of the world's best amateur athletes. The opening ceremonies for the summer Olympic games were starting the next day, and all the athletes and volunteers had to sign in at the desk. Joe, his brother, Frank, and Joe's girlfriend, Vanessa Bender, were part of the 45,000-member summer Olympics volunteer squad. They had driven the Hardys' van nearly nine hundred miles to get to Atlanta, Georgia, where the games were being held. As far as Joe was concerned, it was a total thrill to be here among so many talented competitors.

"I demand to see someone in authority," the man continued. "These people should be kicked out of here now!" He gestured wildly at a group of athletes behind him in line, knocking a cardboard sign off its easel. The sign toppled into Joe.

"Hey, watch out!" Joe cried as he bent down to pick up the sign. Carefully, he placed the sign back on its easel. What is this guy's story? he wondered.

"What's going on?" Frank asked as he stepped up to Joe. Frank was eighteen, a year older than Joe.

"Apparently, Steroid Sam here didn't get the room he wanted," Joe muttered.

"Well, are you going to do something about this situation or not?" The well-built athlete leaned toward the clerk, a menacing expression on his face.

"I'm sorry, sir," the woman said. "There isn't anything—"

"Give it up, Kirov." A wiry guy in line spoke up suddenly. He was about Frank's age and had a shaved head. "We have just as much right to be here as you do. Your people do not rule us at home, and you do not rule us here." He spoke with a slight accent.

"You little worm." The big man sneered. "We will crush you here at the Olympics and then crush you again when we return to our homeland." He took a step toward the other man and cocked a fist.

"Just hold on there," Joe called out, approaching the burly athlete. "These are the Olympic games, remember? Everyone's supposed to cooperate."

The big man looked around the crowded room. Most of the athletes were listening to the angry confrontation. Finally, the huge athlete let his fist drop and narrowed his eyes at Joe. "I will remember your face," he growled. Then he turned around, grabbed his registration slip, and stormed off to the elevators.

Vanessa hurried over. "The Hulk looked pretty mad, Joe. You'd better watch your step."

"He's nothing but a bully." The wiry young man with the shaved head stepped forward and offered his hand. "I'm Turrell Lavrin," he said. "My friends call me Terry. I run the hundred meters and anchor the relay team for the country of Cyrena."

Joe nodded. Cyrena was a small country in the Balkans, and he'd heard they had a strong track and field team. "What's the deal with Muscles?" he asked.

"He is a shot-putter named Vlad Kirov from Gurnistan," Terry said. "The leaders of Gurnistan have tried to regain control of my country since we declared independence five years ago." He sighed. "I'd hoped we could forget politics—at least for these two weeks during the Olympics." Terry then said he had to rejoin his team. "They count on me for interpreting. I hope to see you later." He smiled at the three teenagers before joining his team at the registration desk.

Vanessa, Frank, and Joe stepped up to another desk to complete their check-in process. Joe and Frank had volunteered to handle equipment for the track and field competitions. Because of her computer skills, Vanessa was working in the broadcasting center.

"Looks like we're in Building One, and you're in Six," Frank said to Vanessa, checking their registration slips.

"The sooner I'm settled, the better," she said. Her ash blond hair fell away from her shoulders as she reached for her duffel bag. "I'm exhausted."

"I'll walk Vanessa over to Building Six and meet you back in our room," Joe said.

"Sounds good," Frank replied. "I'm ready for some rest, too. See you later, Vanessa."

4

The Olympic Village complex was teeming with people from almost every nation around the world. As Joe walked Vanessa to her dorm, he noticed hundreds of security officers, media people, and famous athletes.

"Look." Joe nudged Vanessa. "There's Mark Johnson, U.S. four-hundred-meter champion, and he's talking to Pablo Acosta from Spain, the top three-meter diver in the world." He paused to look ahead of them. "And there's that girl from the West Coast, Sherry Meyers. She's a gold medal contender in all-around gymnastics."

"Joe Hardy, you're in jock heaven," Vanessa observed with a smile.

"You've got that right, Vanessa. Seeing the Olympics four years ago was great. But this time, we're *working* it, behind the scenes, where the action is!"

They found Vanessa's building at the end of the row of a half-dozen twelve-story brick buildings. The dorms lined a large, grassy park called the Olympic Commons.

Joe helped Vanessa get settled, then headed back to Building One and his room for a nap. They were due at a meeting for all volunteers in two hours—plenty of time to catch a few Z's.

At four o'clock the Hardys joined a few hundred other volunteers in a large meeting room in Building One. Joe and Frank called hello to several volunteers they'd met in the spring during the intensive training camp.

Then they dropped down on chairs to listen to Kevin O'Malley, the chief of volunteers. He welcomed them to the one hundredth anniversary of the games, then told them where to pick up their assignments and their green-and-tan uniforms.

As Frank and Joe selected their jackets, pants, shirts, shorts, caps, and visors, they heard a familiar voice.

"Welcome back to Atlanta, y'all." It was Carleton Fisher, a twenty-year-old who lived in Georgia. The Hardys had met him during the training session. "You still in track and field?"

Frank nodded. "Pole vaulting. How about you?"

"I'm in pole vaulting myself," Carleton said.

"You are?" Joe was surprised. "I thought you said you'd be working archery."

Carleton plopped a visor on his head. "Changed my mind. So how's Vanessa?" He winked at Joe. "I can't wait to see *her* again."

"You'll see her soon enough." Joe turned abruptly to his brother. "Come on, Frank. Let's get something to eat."

Frank followed him out of the dorm. "I can't stand that guy," Joe muttered. "Remember how he kept coming on to Vanessa during training camp?"

Frank nodded. "How could I possibly forget how mad you got?"

Joe tried to put Carleton out of his mind as the Hardys walked across the Commons to the Discus, a pizza place in the Village International Zone where they'd arranged to meet Vanessa. The Zone was filled with shops, arcades, restaurants, and entertainment facilities for residents, guests, and VIPs.

Vanessa was already there. "We just had our orientation session in the broadcasting center," she told them as they sat at the table. Her blue eyes glowed with excitement. "The place is fantastic. The technology is unbelievable, and it never shuts down. During the games, it will stay open twenty-four hours a day."

Frank and Joe filled her in on their assignments. "We ran into a friend of yours," Frank added, picking up a slice of the pizza she had ordered.

"Yeah, Carleton Fisher sends his regards." Joe scowled. "He's in pole vaulting, too."

"Hey, he's not so bad," Vanessa said. "But why is he staying in the Village? I thought he lived in Atlanta."

"Maybe they want the volunteers to stay together," Joe said. "Lucky us."

Vanessa couldn't stop talking about the

7

state-of-the-art broadcasting center. "The media setup is a hacker's dream," she went on. "It's practically a whole village in itself. They have food vendors, supply stores, a post office, delivery and rental services, video and audio libraries right there—even a place to nap."

"Sounds awesome," Joe said. "Is that where you'll be for the opening ceremonies tomorrow night?"

She nodded. "I'm working the audio room. How about you guys?"

"We're part of the show," Joe mumbled around a mouthful of pizza.

"One part of the ceremony is a preview of the twenty-first-century games," Frank explained. "It's called the Intergalactic Olympics."

"We're playing Martians," Joe said.

"I always knew you were from outer space," Vanessa said, grinning.

"Very funny." Joe downed the last of the soda. "Actually, the show sounds cool. An astronaut is flying into the stadium with one of those jet-powered backpacks. Now, that's the role I'd like!"

The next morning Frank and Joe were up early. Their first job as volunteers was to attend a rehearsal for the opening ceremonies. They made a quick stop at the Village mess hall.

Frank and Joe heaped their plates with food, then looked around for a table.

"Joe! Frank!"

Terry Lavrin was sitting at a round table with three young men, all with shaved heads and dressed in their country's bright blue-and-gold uniforms. "Come sit with us, please," Terry called.

The Hardys went over to the table and sat down.

"Meet my teammates," Terry said. "These are the runners for Cyrena. Bozi does the four-hundred meters, Datko the five-thousand meters, and Raisal the one-hundred and two-hundred meters. We are also a superior relay team," Terry added. "See? We have aerodynamic heads." He rubbed his hand over his smooth scalp. The rest of the team followed suit, nodding and laughing.

"I did not ask you yesterday," Terry said as he sliced a peach with a small silver knife. "What are your sports?"

"Actually, we're not athletes," Frank said. "We're working here as Olympic volunteers."

A short, stocky man approached the table. "Ah, volunteers. What would we do without you?"

"This is our coach, Biron Masily." Terry quickly introduced the Hardys.

After breakfast, Frank and Joe stood up and

wished the Cyrenians luck. Then they left to board the volunteers' shuttle to Olympic Stadium for the opening ceremonies rehearsal.

The approach to the stadium was a long, colorful walkway. Vendors hawked Olympic pins and souvenirs, as well as food and newspapers. Banners representing various sports and nations hung along the walls of the corridor.

"This is amazing," Joe said.

Frank nodded in agreement. Being part of a huge event like the Olympics was the chance of a lifetime.

The Hardys joined the other volunteers on the field for the practice session. A choreographer explained that all the "aliens" would hold mock track-and-field equipment as props. Their job was to pantomime various sports while singers and dancers performed on a raised stage in the middle of the stadium.

After a few run-throughs, the volunteers were finished rehearsing. They gathered in a huge locker room under the stadium to get their costumes.

Frank and Joe were issued the Martians' bright red-and-orange jumpsuits. The eerie yellow masks that went with them had high, arched foreheads and bulging eyes but no ears or noses. Frank grabbed his prop—a three-foot-long plastic javelin—and pretended to jab Joe.

"Hey, watch it." Joe jabbed him back. "I've got one, too."

By now the locker room was crowded with weird-looking aliens. There were creatures from Venus in shiny purple outfits holding foam shots for shot-putting. Mock athletes from Jupiter wore bright yellow and held flat plastic discuses.

"Look at our friend from Neptune," Frank remarked. Carleton Fisher was dressed in the Neptunians' blue-and-green jumpsuit and carrying a plastic bow and arrow.

"Mars can take Neptune any day," Joe said.

Frank laughed. "Hey, don't take this Intergalactic Olympics stuff too seriously," he said.

Before Joe could reply, the choreographer clapped his hands. "Okay, aliens. I'll see you back here at four. Don't be late."

The Hardys packed up their costumes and spent the rest of the day exploring the Zone.

By five o'clock that afternoon, Olympic Stadium was packed with 85,000 spectators.

Joe and Frank climbed into the stands with the other aliens in costumes. The group of volunteers was sitting at the far end of the field. When it was time for them to perform, they were all supposed to hustle onto the field.

Joe stared at the sea of faces from around the world. TV cameras were everywhere.

Suddenly, trumpets sounded, hushing the crowd. The opening ceremonies were about to begin.

The Olympic band marched in, playing an electrifying fanfare. Next came the Olympic flag, the same one used at every Olympic games since 1920.

From their seats, Frank and Joe watched the parade of teams from each participating country. As always, Greece was first, followed by the rest of the countries in alphabetical order.

"The U.S. comes last," Frank explained. "Because we're the host country."

Each of the two hundred teams marched proudly behind its country's flag, waving madly to the fans above.

The Hardys joined the chant of "U-S-A, U-S-A" as the Americans entered last.

Finally, the games were declared open by the president of the International Olympic Committee, and the Olympic torch arrived. Holding the flame high, the torchbearer ascended the steps to the great cauldron. He turned east, west, north, then south before dipping the propane-fueled torch in the cauldron. A cheer rang out as the fire danced around the rim of the bowl, then ignited into a perfect flame in the center.

After the Olympic oaths were taken, Joe glanced at the sky. It was nearly time for the astronaut's dramatic entrance, the part of the show he'd been waiting for.

A moment later the astronaut zoomed into view, sailing over the edge of the stadium toward the large paper bull's-eye in the center of the field. Joe watched him regulate his speed with hand controls connected to the jet-powered backpack.

"Awesome," he said to Frank. "Someday I'd like to try—"

A high-pitched sound came from behind Joe in the stands, interrupting him. He glanced back toward the "aliens" saluting the astronaut with their fake bows, discuses, and javelins.

"What was that?" he murmured. Carleton, who was perched on the back of the stadium wall, waved his bow.

Joe frowned and turned back toward the stadium.

"Oh, no!" Frank cried. The astronaut's body stiffened for a second before going completely limp.

"He's in trouble!" somebody shouted.

Sure enough, the astronaut's hands dropped off the controls, and his helmet pitched forward. The jetpack flier was plummeting downward, spiraling out of control!

Chapter

2

As THE JETPACK FLIER plunged toward the stands, horrified screams filled the air. The mass of "aliens" in the front section of the bleachers scrambled out of the way as the out-of-control astronaut crashed down.

Instantly, a knot of security officers charged across the field. From another direction an ambulance zoomed toward the fallen astronaut. Joe felt the adrenaline pumping through him. Was the guy okay? What an unbelievable scene!

Before Joe could spring into action, the choreographer who'd been working with the volunteers addressed the performers. "Come on," he barked. "We've got to keep the show going."

The volunteers quickly began filing onto the field.

Joe grabbed his brother's arm. "Wait, Frank. Right before that guy lost control, I heard something—a whistling sound. It sounded like it came from the last row. Let's check it out."

The Hardys peeled off their masks and jammed them inside their Martian jumpsuits.

They pushed through the crowd and made their way up to the last row. Most of the seats were empty now. The brothers scanned the floor for possible clues.

"Hey, what's this?" Frank pointed at the ground. Two red-and-blue-striped ropes snaked out from under a seat and hung over the back wall of the stands.

"That's a threaded figure eight," Joe said as he stared at the knot tied to a support under a seat. "We use them in rock climbing."

Frank jumped up onto the bench in the last row and looked over the wall. The ropes led down to an enclosed maintenance area. Several Dumpsters sat on the ground. A large door in the far wall allowed trucks to empty the Dumpsters from the parking lot.

"Look!" Joe saw a short, wiry figure dressed in a purple costume dash out from behind a Dumpster. He bolted through a door that led into the parking lot.

"Somebody's in a hurry," Frank said.

15

"Remember the rappelling techniques we learned from rock climbing?" Joe said. "They're about to come in handy."

Joe grabbed one of the ropes and quickly began to lower himself. Frank followed. They rappelled down the back of the stands into the Dumpster area, pushing off the wall with their feet every twenty feet or so. Finally, they reached the ground and ran toward the door. Ahead of them, in the parking lot, they saw a flash of purple. The Venusian ducked behind a row of cars, then disappeared

"Let's split up," Frank said. Joe nodded and raced to the left.

Frank glanced up. A medical helicopter hovered above the stadium, then dropped down for a landing on the field. Help for the astronaut had arrived very quickly. Frank hoped he'd be okay.

He stood still for a moment, waiting for the noise from the chopper to die down. Then he heard a sound nearby—the crunch of gravel in the next row over. He dropped to the ground, looking under the parked vehicles. About four cars ahead, he caught another glimpse of the shiny purple costume.

Frank crept forward. Ahead of him, he heard a car door open. He popped up and saw the door of a Jeep slam shut.

"Frank," Joe called from ten yards behind. "It's the Venusian. He's in that Jeep!"

"Right," Frank said. The engine started, and the vehicle barreled out of the row. As the Jeep sped by, Frank saw the driver peel off the hooded mask. For a split second, his eyes met the driver's. The Venusian looked startled, then lunged for a pair of wraparound shades from the dashboard. The car tore out of the lot, leaving behind a cloud of dust.

Frank turned to Joe. "It was a girl," he said. "She has really short hair, almost a buzz cut. And big eyes. She's pretty."

Frank walked over to check the space where the Jeep had been parked. He picked up a cardboard disk about the size of a quarter. It had the number thirteen printed inside a white triangle with white stripes. At the top of the disk was a small hole with a tear.

"What's that?" Joe asked.

"I don't know—could be garbage." Frank shrugged.

"Or it could have been dropped by the Venusian," Joe pointed out.

"Or by one of the other thousands of people who parked here." Frank slipped the cardboard disk into the wristband of his costume. "I'll take it with us, just in case."

* * *

The Hardys hurried back inside the stadium, eager to find out about the astronaut. They flashed their badges at the volunteers' entrance. A few people, mostly police and security officials, still milled around the area where the astronaut had fallen. But the chopper was gone, and the panic seemed to have subsided. Most of the spectators were back in their seats, waiting for the show to begin again.

"Let's go make a report to security," Frank said. The Hardys went to the security post at the end of the stadium and introduced themselves to Officer Joe Heiser. He listened to their story, then radioed another policeman, Detective Lyle Posten.

"We found this," Frank told the two men. He pulled the cardboard disk out of his sleeve.

Detective Posten took a look at the small disk, then said, "We'll check it out," in his southern drawl. "Show us where you found the ropes."

The Hardys led the investigators back up to the last row of volunteers' stands.

"Someone wanted to make a quick getaway," Detective Posten said grimly. "There's a good chance it's the person who launched the attack on the astronaut."

"Attack? What are you talking about?" Joe said.

"It looks like the astronaut was shot," Posten said.

Frank and Joe exchanged glances. So that was what the low whistling sound was. Someone had fired at the astronaut, then bolted.

"How is he?" Joe asked.

"Don't know for sure," Officer Heiser said.

"The folks at University Hospital handle the medical reports," Detective Posten added abruptly.

By the time the officers had removed the ropes and finished questioning the Hardys, the aliens' production number was half over.

"Vanessa's going to be disappointed she didn't get to see us perform," Joe said.

"As long as we missed most of our debut, we might as well cut out of here," Frank replied. "Maybe we can hit the hospital and see what we can find out."

Joe quickly agreed. "We'd better ditch the costumes first."

At field level they ducked into one of the tunnels that led to the huge area below the stadium. Inside were locker rooms, showers, offices, meeting rooms, and storage areas.

As they descended, the sounds from outside grew muffled. The Hardys could hear their own footsteps echoing through the long tunnel.

"I was just thinking," Frank began. "There

were two ropes, but we saw only one person running from the Dumpster shed."

"You're right," Joe said. "Do you think two people were involved?"

"Definitely." Frank nodded. "Why else would there be two ropes?"

"Carleton was in the back row, wasn't he?" Joe said. "He and some of the other aliens were sitting on the wall when the astronaut was shot."

"Maybe he can help us out," Frank said. "He might have noticed something back there."

Joe nodded. "Sounds good. So far, our only clue is that cardboard disk."

"That disk is bugging me," said Frank. "There's something familiar about that white-striped triangle, but I can't figure out what it is."

They walked deeper into the tunnel, heading for the room where volunteers were supposed to drop off their costumes. Suddenly, Frank stopped and grabbed Joe's arm, motioning for him to be quiet.

Then Joe heard it, too—footsteps echoing along the tunnel behind them. The footsteps stopped.

Six feet away from the Hardys, a door stood open. Frank nodded toward it, and the two brothers tiptoed over to the dark room.

Joe felt his pulse pick up as the footsteps outside drew nearer. He peeked out through the crack in the open door.

A huge shadow loomed against the far wall. As the man himself came into view, Joe saw he was big and bulky. He wore a dark running suit and the eerie blue-and-green mask of a Neptunian. In his hand was a shiny black automatic pistol.

Joe drew back abruptly. His sudden movement made the door creak loudly. The hulking figure in the hallway looked around, then whirled toward the open door. Now his black pistol was pointing directly at the Hardys.

Chapter

3

FRANK LUNGED FOR THE DOOR and slammed it shut. Then he locked it.

Joe glanced around the room. It looked like a meeting room, with nothing much in it besides some folding chairs. There were no windows for escape and nothing they could use as weapons to defend themselves.

The Hardys watched the long, L-shaped door handle turn downward. It jiggled and jerked violently for a couple of seconds, then there was a pause.

Something slammed against the door, again and again. Whoever was out there was trying to barrel through the locked door!

Frank and Joe backed away. Joe picked up

a chair, ready to throw it when the door crashed open.

"You there." A man's voice echoed through the tunnel. "That's not the dressing room. The aliens are supposed to return costumes across the hall."

"Okay," another voice replied. There was a pause, and then Joe and Frank heard footsteps leading away from the door.

Joe let out his breath. "Saved in the nick of time."

Frank slowly unlocked the door. The corridor was empty.

"Let's look around and see if we can find anybody. Be careful; the guy had a gun," Frank said.

Volunteers dressed in alien suits began filing into the tunnel. As Frank and Joe headed for the dressing room, Carleton sauntered toward them. He was already in street clothes, his costume tucked under his arm.

"What happened to you two?" he asked. "You took off when the guy was shot. Where'd you go?"

"How do you know he was shot?" Frank asked, giving Carleton a sharp look.

"Everybody's talking about it," Carleton said with a shrug. "I heard it was a high-powered rifle. Dropped the guy like a pigeon with buckshot."

23

"What about you, Carleton?" Joe demanded, watching him closely. "How did you change so quickly?"

"Uh," Carleton began, "I figured I'd duck the singing and dancing stuff at the end. That's not my style, really." The Hardys followed him as he dropped his costume into a large bin outside the dressing room.

"You were in the top row of the stands," Joe said. "Did you see anything strange up there?"

"Anything strange?" Carleton grinned. "I was surrounded by aliens waving bows, shot puts, and javelins. That's what I call strange."

"How about anything *suspicious?*" Frank asked. "Anyone who wasn't supposed to be there, for instance?"

"No way," Carleton said. He shoved his mask into a duffel bag. "Not from where I sat. Anyway, who could tell? Everyone was in costume. Maybe the shot came from the press box behind us."

"Not very likely," Joe muttered.

"Well, see y'all later," Carleton said. "Tomorrow morning's the pole vault trials. You think tonight was exciting, wait until then. Going to be one wild time out there." He left quickly.

The Hardys ditched their costumes, then

looked around for signs of the Neptunian who'd followed them.

"Do you think it was Carleton?" Joe asked.

Frank shrugged. "You got a better look at the guy, but my guess is no. Whoever it was had a solid build."

A few minutes later the Hardys left the stadium and crossed the street to a glass-enclosed station. A sleek train pulled in, and they jumped aboard. Olympic volunteers could ride for free.

The train wove through the center of the city. The Hardys got off at the university where the hospital was located. They wanted to check on the condition of the wounded astronaut.

The hospital lobby was packed with reporters, photographers, and other media people. A man with a clipboard stood behind a huge tangle of microphones, dodging reporters' questions.

Through the crowd, Joe spotted Vanessa's ash blond hair up front. The Hardys threaded their way toward her.

"I wondered if we'd find you here," Joe whispered.

"Wouldn't miss it," Vanessa answered, reaching out to adjust one of the mikes. "Wasn't that awful?"

"Any word on what happened?" Frank asked softly. "Is the astronaut okay?"

"Just a lot of smoke so far," Vanessa said. "I can't tell whether the Olympics people *really* don't know anything, or if they do and they're keeping it quiet. There haven't been any doctors out here yet—just this press relations guy from the hospital."

A reporter suddenly spoke up. He had a thick accent. "Ladies and gentlemen, I am the official representative of the Cyrenian Press Agency. The entire world should be aware of Gurnistan's terrorist actions." The bustling room quickly fell silent as he went on. "Today's attack is clearly another in a series of Gurnistani terrorist actions against the peaceful people of Cyrenia. We Cyrenians demand that the Gurnistani assassin who felled our countryman be brought to justice."

All around the room, reporters began scribbling notes. Strobe lights flashed.

"Hold on, everybody," the hospital spokesman said. "The facts aren't in yet. It's too early to declare this attack a terrorist act." He tucked his clipboard under his arm and said, "More information will be released as it becomes available." Then he turned quickly to leave the room.

The reporters rapidly descended on the man from Cyrena.

"Let's get out of here," Frank said. "Something tells me it's going to be a long wait to get the real story."

Joe grabbed Vanessa's hand, and they followed Frank out of the hospital. The three hopped a train to the Village.

On the way, the Hardys filled Vanessa in about their evening.

"Those ropes were kern mantles," Joe said. "Probably eleven millimeters, serious rock-climbing equipment."

"Whoever rigged them knew what they were doing," Frank added. "They weren't taking any chances on getting to the bottom safely."

"How do you suppose they got them up there without anyone seeing them?" Vanessa asked.

"They could easily have been smuggled up under those costumes," Frank said. "The jumpsuits are so loose, nobody would notice."

"And if you're experienced with ropes, you can tie those knots quickly," Joe said. "Or maybe the ropes were there the whole time. Maybe the guys sitting on the wall were sitting on the ropes to hide them."

"Any theories in the broadcasting center about who did it?" Frank asked Vanessa as they sped under the downtown district.

"Plenty," she answered. "Everybody started reviewing the videotapes right after it happened. Some people were saying that the astronaut had a heart attack or seizure or something, but most of them figure it was like the guy from Cyrena said—terrorists. What's going on between those two countries, anyway?"

"Gurnistan and Cyrena are in the Balkans," Frank said. "They used to be one country, then Cyrena separated, and they had a civil war. They're still jockeying for territory."

"Carleton said he heard the jetpack flier was shot with a rifle," Joe told Vanessa.

"That doesn't make sense," Frank said. "You could maybe stash a rifle under your costume, but there's no way you could stand up and fire without being noticed in that crowd. If he was shot, it wasn't with a rifle."

"How come the astronaut was from Cyrena, anyway?" Joe asked. "It seems odd he wasn't American—we're the host country."

"I checked that out," Vanessa said. "The Olympic Committee held a competition in Rome six months ago. People were invited to try out—show off their maneuvers and skill with the jetpack. The Cyrenian won the honor of flying at the Olympics. It was all kept quiet because the astronaut was supposed to be a big surprise for the crowd."

"I wonder if there's anything new on the guy's condition," Frank said.

"I can check it out," Vanessa said as they

approached the main gate. "There's a branch of the press center here in the Village, over by the Slam Dunk dance club."

"Can you get in there?" Frank asked.

"Sure. All I have to do is show my press pass," Vanessa said. "I can check directly with the hospital. I got its E-mail number. I've worked out some decoding I'd like to try on their records database. I'll plug my computer into theirs and see what I can pick up."

"I knew it was a smart move to bring along a hacker," Frank said with a grin.

Their badges were scrutinized carefully before they were allowed onto the Village campus. Frank looked at the double chain fence ringing the Village and the surveillance cameras scanning the area. He wondered if this extra security would be enough to deter future attacks.

"We'll wait for you in the Slam Dunk," Joe told Vanessa. With a wave, she jogged off to the press center.

Lots of people were inside the Slam Dunk, but only a few couples were dancing. Most gathered in small groups, talking quietly with worried expressions about the astronaut's crash.

"We've got to get to the bottom of this, Joe," Frank said as they checked out the scene. "We can't let it destroy the Olympics."

For the next few minutes, they reviewed what they'd discovered so far: Probably two people had escaped from the stadium by rope. They had two suspects, the big guy who followed them into the tunnel and a girl with a buzz cut who was dressed as a Venusian. Plus, there was the cardboard disk with the number thirteen.

"Don't forget Carleton Fisher," Joe added.

"Right," Frank replied. "He acted a little strange tonight."

Vanessa rushed toward them a short while later. "I got some big news on the flier," she said breathlessly. "He's probably going to be all right, but he was definitely shot."

"With what?" Frank asked.

"Well, no one has said officially, but I got this from the hospital computer records." She lowered her voice. "It's not supposed to be released yet. Take a look." She handed Joe a piece of paper.

Frank read over his brother's shoulder.

"Unbelievable," Joe muttered as he read the printout. "No wonder everyone had trouble figuring out what hit this guy."

Chapter

4

JOE BEGAN TO READ the note aloud: "'A six-inch bolt, threaded steel tip, anodized gold, extracted at 8:23 P.M.'" Joe looked at his brother. "A bolt, Frank. The guy must have been shot with a crossbow!"

"Of course," Frank said. "Crossbows don't shoot arrows, they shoot bolts. Sort of like a steel dart, only more lethal." He frowned. "But the bolt was only six inches? That's small for a crossbow."

"Maybe it was a *pistol* crossbow," Joe said. "They're the perfect size. Even with a crosshair target scope attached, you could hide one under those alien costumes."

"One person could smuggle in the weapon,"

Frank added, "while the other brings in the ropes." He turned to his brother's girlfriend. "Vanessa, you've done archery. Isn't there something called a self-cocking pistol cross-bow?"

"Yes," she answered. "They're pretty pow-erful. I'd hate to be a target of one of those."

Frank pictured the stands earlier that night. "Those aliens from Neptune had plastic bows," he remarked. "Nobody would have noticed a pistol crossbow."

"An experienced shooter could definitely pull that off," Joe said. He started acting out the procedure. "Jump up, pull out the cross-bow—already loaded and cocked—wave it a few seconds, pull it in to set the scope on the flier, pull the trigger, and slip the crossbow back into your costume." The whole thing took about four seconds.

"The accomplice could have shielded the shooter," Frank said. "If they were in the last row, no one was behind them to see what they were doing."

"Everyone was looking up anyway, right?" Vanessa said. "Watching the astronaut."

Frank and Joe agreed. "Okay, so maybe we figured out the 'how,' " Joe said. "Now, what about the 'who' and 'why'?"

Frank checked his watch. It was ten o'clock. "Let's visit the Cyrenian runners," he said.

"Their events don't start for two days, so they're probably not in bed early. They seem like our best lead at this point."

The three left the dance club and went straight to Building One. They showed the checkpoint guard their residence passes and went up to Frank and Joe's room, where Joe called Terry.

"It is good to hear from my new American friends," Terry said. "We are so angry. The flying astronaut is our countryman. We fear that the terrorist act that felled him won't be the last."

"That's what we want to talk to you about, Terry," Joe said. "I know it's late, but can we get together for a few minutes? We'd like to ask you a few questions."

"Of course," Terry said. "I will not sleep until I hear about our comrade, anyway. Come to my room. I am at the end on the fifth floor. I will tell the guards you are coming. The Olympic Committee posted extra security after the assault."

The Hardys and Vanessa were in Terry's room within minutes.

"Have you heard that the astronaut was shot?" Frank asked.

Terry nodded, his dark eyes sparked with anger. "It was the Gurnistanis. A typical assault on an innocent man."

"Could it have been a woman?" Frank asked. He described the woman he'd seen in the parking lot. "She's young and pretty, and her hair is cut very short."

Terry hesitated, then said, "The underground revolutionaries in our country wear their hair extremely short—almost shaved like ours." He ran his palm over his smooth head.

"Even the women?" Frank asked.

"Yes." Terry nodded. "But one of our own would never do such a thing—shoot a comrade down."

"How about the shot-putter who was hassling you yesterday when we registered?" Joe asked. "Could he have anything to do with it?"

"I would not put anything past a Gurnistani. They are all capable of murder. But Kirov is not so smart. He probably doesn't have the ability to do anything so calculated. No, it was likely done by paid assassins posing as athletes."

"Could it have been a personal attack on the astronaut?" Frank asked.

"I do not think so. He has no political connections. The attack was just another way for the Gurnistani government to show its power and its contempt for world opinion." Terry stared at the Hardys for a second. "I mean no offense, but why are you taking an interest in our small country?"

Joe and Frank exchanged glances.

"Uh—" Joe began.

"Don't be modest, you two," Vanessa spoke up. "Joe and Frank are detectives," she explained. *"Ace* investigators. Their dad is a detective, too. Fenton Hardy is his name."

"This is wonderful news." Terry broke out in a smile for a minute before growing serious again. "You must help us," he pleaded. "For months, the Gurnistanis have warned us that horrible things will happen to our team. The assault on the astronaut is just the beginning, I know it. You must stop them."

"We'll do our best," Frank assured him.

"Terry, do the Gurnistanis or Cyrenians have any volunteers here?" Joe asked.

"Not that I know of. Why?"

"It's a way to get access to the inside of the games," Joe explained.

"Well, I think that's all for now," Frank said. "We'll keep in touch."

The Hardys and Vanessa hurried out of the room and onto the elevator. As the doors closed, Joe said, "We've got to find the girl with the buzz cut."

Frank nodded. "I have another idea. Let's—"

"Check out the videotape from this afternoon?" Vanessa interrupted. She held up her notebook computer by its carrying case handle. "I thought you'd never ask."

Frank and Joe followed her into their room. She set up the computer on one of the desks. "I've been working on these codes since training camp last spring," she said.

"You mean the codes to the broadcasting center?" Frank asked as he watched her log in.

"Exactly," Vanessa said. She punched in a bunch of numbers, then whizzed the mouse around its pad. Within seconds, a video of the opening ceremonies showed up on the small monitor.

"Let's start with just before the jetpack flier came in over the stadium," Frank said.

Vanessa sped up the tape to that spot. There were several shots of the scene from different cameras. They watched the flier zoom in, circle once, then go limp. The Hardys viewed it backward, forward, in slow motion, and then in magnified view.

"There," Frank said suddenly as they ran through the tape for the fourth time. "Stop it right there. See that dark thing in the stands?"

Joe looked at the spot where Frank was pointing, to a tiny black object.

"That could be anything," Vanessa said, "even a tape defect."

"Or it could be the crossbow bolt," Joe said.

"Look." Frank traced a path on the screen.

"That thing came from under the press box at the top of our stands, right about where the ropes were."

Vanessa replayed the segment so Joe could see. As the tape played past that point, something else caught Joe's eye. "Frank, look at the ads!" he cried.

Vanessa froze the shot, and Frank scanned the advertising signs and banners hanging from the front of the stands. One jumped out from the rest—a stylized white triangle with white stripes.

"That cardboard disk I found has the same pattern!" Frank said. "It's the logo for the Stonewall Lodge."

"Maybe that woman from the parking lot is staying there," Joe mused. "The logo could have been torn off a room key or something."

"Where is that disk, anyway?" Vanessa asked.

"We gave it to the security guys," Joe told her.

Vanessa yawned. "Are you guys through with this footage? I'm pretty beat. I want to get some sleep."

Frank and Joe nodded and helped her pack up the computer. "I'll be right back," Joe told Frank. "I'm going to walk Vanessa home."

"I'll be snoring by the time you get back," Frank joked.

It was twelve-thirty when Joe headed back across the Commons from Vanessa's place. Two security officers stood by a small fountain designed in the shape of the five Olympic rings. Joe could hear music blaring from the Zone. People were still streaming in and out of the clubs and shops. Joe yawned. Don't those people need sleep? he thought.

The air was heavy and humid. Joe's mind was on the start of competition the next day, but he snapped to attention the moment he heard footsteps crunch behind him. He dropped down and pretended to tie a shoelace. As he bent over, he stole a glance behind him. No one.

He started home again, feeling wide awake now. All his senses were on alert. A twig snapped behind him. He wheeled around quickly but still saw no one.

Then something else alerted him—static from the security officer's radios. The two officers held their radios to their ears, then hurried away. Joe followed the men toward the security checkpoint near the Zone. I wonder what's happened now, he thought. Maybe . . .

Something was going on.

By the time Joe was aware of someone running up behind him, it was too late. He felt a sudden, hard blow to his right kidney. The impact forced the air out of his lungs, then his legs gave out under him.

Chapter
5

JOE WAS SLAMMED to the ground.

"This is your only warning. Stay out of matters that do not concern you," a low voice growled.

As Joe lay there gasping for air, he saw a bulky figure in dark clothes jog away. He tried to go after the guy, but he couldn't catch his breath. He dropped back down on the grass. A few minutes later, he stood and made his way back to Building One.

"What took you so long?" Frank asked as Joe entered their room.

"I was ambushed," Joe explained. "The guy surprised me big time." He filled Frank in on what had happened.

"Did you get a look at him?" Frank asked.

"It was dark, but I think this guy had the same build as the muscleman who followed us into the tunnel," Joe said. "All I know is, he gave me some karate chop. I feel like a truck ran me over."

"It sounds like one did," his brother replied. "Why don't you get some rest?"

By the time Frank had finished putting away his clothes and brushing his teeth, Joe was sound asleep on the other bed.

In the morning Joe felt better.

"You got quite a bruise," Frank said, checking Joe's back. "You're sure you're up for today?"

"I've had worse hits playing football," Joe said. "The worst part is, I didn't have a chance to slug the guy back."

"You look sore, but you sound like yourself." Frank grinned. "Come on, we'd better hustle."

The Hardys pulled on their Olympic shorts and polo shirts, had a quick breakfast, and headed for Olympic Stadium.

"There y'all are," Carleton called out as they approached. "You cut it pretty close, boys. We start in a half hour."

"So how long have you been here?" Joe asked, adjusting the visor of his volunteer cap.

"Since the stadium opened," Carleton said smugly. "I got here over an hour ago."

Joe ignored Carleton and turned his attention to the field. Several athletes were warming up for the first day of the pole vault trials.

"That's why the pole vault is the toughest event in track and field," he told Frank. He watched one of the vaulters make a practice run up to the takeoff box. "You have to have the upper-body strength of a weightlifter, the legs of a sprinter, and the balance of a gymnast."

"You a vaulter?" Carleton asked before Frank could reply.

Joe nodded. "I've done some."

"How about you, Carleton?" Frank asked.

The southerner shrugged. "Not me. That's one event I don't know anything about." He headed out the locker-room door. "Catch y'all later."

"Not if I can help it," Joe muttered.

"Come on, Joe," said Frank. "Let's find Mr. Hill. He's the guy who's supposed to tell us what to do."

Each sport had a team of volunteers supervised by a volunteer commissioner. The team was divided into squads according to task, and each squad had a leader. There was a law enforcement official, a protocol chairman, a chief medical officer, and managers for equipment, results, and transportation.

The Hardys quickly found the equipment manager, whom they'd met in the spring. Mr. Hill was a retired university coach. "This is it, folks," he was saying to the group of volunteers gathered around him. "The moment you've been training for. Our team is in charge of the athletes' equipment. Remember to follow the rules established by the Olympic Committee, and we can all make our country proud." He reached for his clipboard. "Here are the final assignments. Albright, Cloud, Hayes—you'll handle the locker-room duties. Keep it clean and neat, and make sure the athletes have plenty of supplies. You know the routine."

As the coach continued reading off names, Frank watched the weight throwers warming up at the opposite end of the field. A group of hurdlers practiced alongside the discus and shot-put ring.

"Hardy, Frank." At the mention of his name, Frank looked up. "You and Fisher will man the takeoff box and pit. Hardy, Joe. You'll assist the vaulters with their poles."

"So you're stuck with Carleton," Joe mumbled to Frank after the meeting. "Sorry about that."

"Hey, I can take it," Frank said. "At least I'm at the box—right where the action is."

Joe nodded. Frank was right. That was the best part of the assignment—being able to watch the pole vaulters up close. "See you later," he said. Then he hurried to the area where the athletes grabbed their poles before beginning their approach.

Frank followed Carleton to the pole-vaulting site. The vaulters had to jump over a huge crossbar about eighteen feet high. The pit was where they landed. It consisted of a foam-filled pad that lay beyond the crossbar. In front of the pit was the takeoff box, sometimes called the planting or vaulting box. The vaulters launched into their jumps by jamming their poles into the box and swinging their bodies upward.

"We're supposed to keep the takeoff box clean and free of debris," Carleton said. "And check the pit for tears and holes in the foam pad." Frank knew they were also in charge of getting the crossbar out of the pit when it was knocked down by a vaulter who didn't clear it.

Frank watched as the trials began. Each time a vaulter soared over the crossbar, a section of the crowd cheered. Competitors awaiting their turn paced nervously along the sidelines. As the trials continued, the crossbar was raised higher and higher. Along with the bar, tension was beginning to mount.

Frank held his breath as Chuck Parrish, an American, approached the box. Although the volunteers were asked not to root for any one team, it was hard not to get excited about Parrish, who'd been named the favorite.

Yes! Frank thought as Parrish easily cleared the bar. The first trials ended with the Americans at the top of the qualifying ranks.

Joe was just as excited about the U.S. team. "They're going to do it," he told Frank when they met in the volunteers' locker room at lunchtime. "I know it. That Chuck Parrish is great."

"He's awesome, all right," Frank agreed.

"If he vaults like that during the finals, he'll break the record. It's so cool that we're here to see it."

Frank nodded, then glanced at his watch. "The trials begin again at four-thirty. Let's grab some lunch, then check with those two detectives we met after the astronaut shooting. I think you should tell them about the guy who gave you the kidney chop."

"I can't go," Joe said. "Chuck Parrish missed some practice time yesterday and has a makeup this afternoon. He asked me to hang around for a while and help him with equipment."

"Okay. I'll get in touch with Detective Posten and tell him what happened. Then I'll meet you back here."

Joe nodded. "Sounds good." By the time he got back onto the field, the stands were almost cleared of spectators. Joe watched Parrish take a few easy vaults, then helped him raise the crossbar a foot.

"The world record's over nineteen feet," Joe remarked. "Are you going for it?"

Parrish looked at him, surprised. "Are you a vaulter?"

"Bayport champ and state record holder," Joe admitted.

"Is that right? Let's see how good you are." Parrish threw him one of his backup poles. "I'll spot you a foot and a half." He lowered the crossbar to seventeen feet. "You're up."

Joe took a deep breath. He knew he should warm up a little first, but Parrish was waiting. He looked around nervously before picking up the pole. This was unbelievable. Here he was vaulting in Olympic Stadium with the guy who was supposed to be the best at the sport.

"You get three shots at it, just like in regulation," Parrish said.

Joe nodded, then shook the fiberglass pole a few times to get the feel of it. It felt like four and a half pounds, the same weight as his pole back home.

He walked back until he was about a hundred feet from the takeoff box. Then he carefully placed his right hand on the pole, thumb over the top, and placed his left hand about two feet below his right, with that thumb underneath the pole.

He rocked in place a few times before starting his run. With pole parallel to the ground, Joe sprinted down the vaulter's runway, concentrating on planting the pole in the takeoff box. At the end, he jammed the pole into the box, then swung his body forward. He bent his knees slightly and could feel his body go into a lift as the pole began to snap back up. His back complained a little, but he was committed. There was no going back now.

He pushed into the pole first with his left arm, then with his right. For a few seconds he hung there, completely upside down, the soles of his feet flat to the sky.

Then he let go with his left hand. The momentum continued to carry his body up. His legs were above the crossbar now, and his only connection to the earth was his right hand gripping the end of the vertical pole.

Joe released his grip, and the familiar exhilaration flooded through him. Pole vaulting felt like flying. By now, he was nearly two stories above ground, propelling his body, legs first, over the crossbar. He lifted his arms and hands up quickly to clear the bar.

As he shot down toward the pit, he bent his knees to absorb the impact. Then he landed, rolling onto his back with an "Ooooomph." The pain from his bruise lifted when he opened his eyes. There, shimmering in the sunlight, was the crossbar, still secure between the uprights.

"Yesss!" Joe yelled.

"Not bad." Parrish grinned. "Maybe you should hang up your volunteer's uniform and join the team."

Parrish raised the crossbar a foot and a half, then picked up the pole he'd been using all morning. Joe watched the track star approach the box. His sprinting and planting form were perfect. With a mighty heave, Parrish launched himself upward. As the pole started its snapback, Parrish swung his legs up, using all the force to send him over the crossbar. It looked like a faultless vault.

Then Joe heard a sickening sound, a brittle snap.

Instinctively, he rushed toward the pit. But by the time he got there, he realized he was helpless.

Parrish's pole had snapped in two, leaving the star vaulter upside down and unsupported fifteen feet above the ground.

47

Chapter

6

JOE GASPED as Chuck Parrish crashed into the ground. In his hand, he clutched a severed piece of pole. Parrish rolled over once and lay silently in a heap, one arm jutting out at an unnatural angle.

"Chuck!" Joe rushed over. "Chuck! Can you hear me?"

There was no answer. Joe ran to get Parrish's warmup jacket and covered the injured vaulter.

Parrish opened his eyes and tried to turn his head to look at Joe. "My pole," he mumbled. "What happened?" Then he closed his eyes again and lay still, wincing in pain.

Joe raced to one of the security phones

along the stadium wall and called for help. The emergency technicians arrived quickly. They checked Parrish's vital signs, then splinted his shoulder. One paramedic said he thought Parrish was okay except for a broken collarbone and slight concussion. As they carried him off the field on a stretcher, Joe felt relief but also disappointment. It was over for the U.S. pole-vaulting team.

He gathered up the pieces of the broken pole, along with the backup pole Parrish had lent him. Then he found the cases for the star's poles. Inside one was a tiny key—the one to the equipment locker, Joe guessed. He pocketed the key, then packed up the poles.

By the time Joe reached the locker room, Frank was back. He hadn't been able to find either of the security officers they'd talked to the night before.

Joe told Frank about Parrish. "Look at this." He opened one of the pole cases and showed Frank the short piece of the pole. "What do you know about fiberglass?"

"It's strong, it's flexible—"

"Right. It bends, but it doesn't break," Joe interrupted. "Poles used to be made from wood or bamboo, then steel or aluminum. They've been using fiberglass since the sixties. There has been only one pole break that I know of since then—in 1988, at the games in Seoul, Korea."

Frank stared at Joe. "You're telling me that this pole was tampered with."

"Definitely." Joe pointed to a slight brownish residue on the broken end of the pole. "I don't know what this stuff is. It's not dirt, and it's not good old Georgia clay."

"Let's get a sample." Frank reached for a pole wipe and gently blotted the end of the pole until it smeared the cloth. Then he folded the wipe carefully and put it in his pocket.

"Did Chuck Parrish use this pole this morning?" Frank asked.

"He sure did," Joe said. "I used one of his backups this afternoon. Maybe we should check out the rest of his equipment—I've got the key to his locker."

The Hardys hurried into the pole room, where each team had a long horizontal metal cabinet to stow its vaulting poles.

Joe opened the U.S. cabinet with Chuck Parrish's key. He located a pole case with the monogram CP-USA and pulled it out.

For several minutes, Frank and Joe inspected the additional backup poles along with the one Joe had used that afternoon. There wasn't a mark on any of them.

Joe slipped Parrish's backup poles into their

cases, put them in the pole cabinet, and locked it. He put the key in his wallet.

By the time they'd stored the poles again, news of Parrish's injury had spread among the competitors. The locker room filled with concerned vaulters and volunteers. The other two members of the American team gathered for a quick rally before the trials resumed. Their teammate's injury was devastating. Joe wondered how they were going to cope.

Within a few hours, the answer was clear. The other two Americans failed to qualify.

Joe couldn't hide his disappointment. "Chuck Parrish is the heart and soul of that team," he told Frank. "What a shame."

As they left the stadium, Frank turned to Joe. "Did you see Carleton this afternoon?"

Joe shook his head. "No, why?"

"He didn't show this afternoon." Frank looked Joe in the eyes. "And I'm beginning to think it's no coincidence."

The Hardys met Vanessa for dinner at the Dead Heat, a Mexican place in the Zone.

She'd already heard about Parrish's accident. "It's big news," she told them. "He was the favorite. He even had a big press conference yesterday."

"He told me that," Joe said. "That's why he missed practice yesterday. You know—" Joe suddenly remembered something. "This isn't the first problem with the U.S. team this year. Remember Jay Hamilton?"

"Wasn't he a vaulting star, too?" Vanessa asked. "Got into some trouble last summer?"

"Yep," Joe said. "Olympic trials in Indianapolis. He was thrown off the team for using steroids. He went nuts. Assaulted the coach, got arrested, and spent a month in jail for it."

"I wonder what he's been doing since he got out," Frank said.

Joe shrugged. "I heard his name mentioned in the locker room. I wouldn't be surprised if he's in town."

After they ordered dinner, Frank called Olympic security and left another message for Officer Heiser. Then he tried Detective Posten again—and reached him this time.

Frank sat back down at the table ten minutes later. "Detective Posten wants you to call with a description of the guy who punched you last night, Joe."

"What?" Vanessa's eyebrows went up. "Who punched you?"

"I don't know, but his fist was the size of a bowling ball," Joe said over a huge bite of burrito. "It happened on my way back from your building. Did you tell Detective Posten about the stain on the pole, Frank?"

Frank nodded and took the cloth from his

pocket. He opened it up and showed Vanessa the smear from the broken end of the pole.

"Looks like blood," she commented.

"I don't think so," Frank said. "My guess would be rust."

"Rust?" Vanessa said. "Fiberglass poles don't rust." She dipped her nacho into some hot salsa.

"But saws do," Joe said. "I'm betting that the tool used to cut through the pole made this mark. Somebody should check the rest of the poles and see if anyone else was targeted beside Chuck Parrish."

"That's what Detective Posten said," Frank answered. "They're going to have security check all the poles, not just the U.S. ones."

"Did you call Carleton Fisher?" Joe asked.

"There was no answer in his room," Frank said. "Maybe you two can track him down after dinner. I'll go talk to the American vaulters."

"It's nine o'clock," Joe said, checking his watch. "Let's meet at the Starting Kick about eleven." Then he turned to Vanessa. "I've been wondering why Carleton bothers to stay here when he lives nearby. Maybe it's time to check out that dude's home base."

After dinner Frank left the Zone and walked across the Commons toward Building Five, where the U.S. vaulting team was staying. He found the two vaulters and their coach in one of the meeting rooms. They were all still upset about Chuck Parrish. The coach was doing his best to raise the younger men's spirits.

Frank asked if any of them had seen anything odd at the field or in the locker or equipment rooms. "No," they said.

"Whatever happened to Jay Hamilton?" Frank asked. "Have you seen him around?"

"He hasn't shown his face around the team since he got out of jail," said a tall guy with the name Edwards stitched on his warmup jacket. "I heard that somebody on the volleyball team saw him out at Stone Mountain yesterday."

A short while later, Frank thanked them and left, checking his watch on the way out of the building. More than an hour had passed since Joe and Vanessa had left to check out Carleton's house.

Frank went back to Building One to check for messages. Maybe Carleton or Officer Heiser had called.

But there were no messages. He headed back to the Zone and the Starting Kick.

On the way, he heard a heavily accented voice call out from behind.

"Frank, Frank Hardy."

Frank turned. Terry Lavrin's coach waved madly, then started toward him.

"Hello, Coach Masily," Frank said.

"I must talk to you, Frank. Terry told me of your discussion with him last night." The coach gripped Frank's arm tightly. "It's important that we talk."

"Okay." Frank scanned the area and spotted an empty bench. "Let's sit down over there."

But Coach Masily couldn't wait another minute. "I have seen the assassins," he hissed. "I know who they are." He loosened his grip and started toward the residence halls. "Come with me. Now! I will show you the faces of these monsters."

Coach Masily stepped off the curb and started across the road in front of the dorms.

Frank was about to follow when he heard the squeal of tires and an engine revving.

A large dark blue van was bearing down on them.

Chapter

7

THE VAN'S ENGINE ROARED as the big vehicle hurtled toward Frank and the Cyrenian coach.

"Hey, watch out!" someone yelled.

Several others walking along the Commons froze in horror.

Frank's survival instinct kicked into high gear. He had time for only one move—and it had to be a good one.

He made a swift grab for Coach Masily's arm and dove toward the opposite curb. But the coach panicked and flailed both his arms.

In the nick of time, Frank reached the curb, but the coach was still in the path of the oncoming van. Then Frank heard a loud thud and an ear-splitting scream. Before he could look to see what had happened, his head smacked into an iron lamppost.

He felt a sharp pain before everything went black.

"This can't be it," Joe insisted as he and Vanessa pulled up in front of a dark house.

"This *is* it," Vanessa told him again. "Seven-eight-nine Clay Hollow Drive, home of Carleton Fisher."

Joe shook his head. The lawn was overgrown with weeds, and there was a For Sale sign nailed to the front porch. "It looks like no one's lived here for a long time."

"Wait a minute, maybe I copied down the wrong address," Vanessa said. She accessed the volunteer database with her laptop computer. The same address turned up.

"Come on, let's ask the neighbors," Joe said. They hopped out and went next door to Number 791. Their knock was answered almost immediately by a smiling young man.

"The Fishers?" the man said. "Sure, we knew them, but they haven't lived next door for over a year now."

"Moved south," added a young woman who stood up from the couch in the living room and joined them at the door. "To Pensacola, Florida."

"Plenty of people have looked at the

house," the young man said, "but no buyers yet. Are you two interested?"

"Not yet," Vanessa said with a grin. "But thanks anyway."

"How about Carleton Fisher? Have you seen him?" asked Joe.

"Nope," the woman said. "Not since the family moved."

Back on the street, Joe shook his head. "What kind of scam is Fisher pulling? Why is he using an old address?"

They were both quiet as they drove back to the Village. Finally, Vanessa said, "I don't really understand why you suspect Carleton. What motive would he have for attacking the astronaut or sabotaging an American pole vaulter?"

"He was sitting in the stands when the bolt was fired," Joe said. "And he was working the pole-vaulting event this morning."

"So were lots of volunteers," Vanessa pointed out. "There were thousands of people around today at the track and at the ceremonies yesterday. I'm worried you just have it in for him."

"I admit I don't like him," Joe said. "But there are several unanswered questions about him. Like, why did he lie about his address? And where was he all afternoon when he was supposed to be helping Frank? Not to mention the very weird fact that he didn't see anything suspicious at the opening ceremonies."

Vanessa shook her head. "Why would Carleton Fisher shoot the Cyrenian jetpack flier?" she asked again. "It makes no sense."

"I don't know why, but I do know from volunteers' training camp that he has experience in archery. He was all set to help in the archery center. So why'd he suddenly change to pole vaulting?"

"It's still not much to go on," Vanessa said.

"That's why we're going to his room right now and see if we can find out anything else," Joe said.

"What about the Gurnistanis? Terry Lavrin's pretty sure they're behind the terrorist attack."

"Maybe Carleton's hooked up with them," Joe said. "Let's just go check out his room."

"What if he's home?"

"Then we'll invite ourselves in for a soda or something. Just follow my lead."

Joe parked in the Village residents' parking lot behind Building One. Then he went to the back of the van and took his lock pick and a small flashlight out of the concealed floor compartment that contained some of the Hardys' detective equipment.

The side doors were locked. Joe and Vanessa walked around to the front of the building and stepped through the entryway. The hall was clear. As they walked to Room 117, they could hear rock music filtering out from one of the rooms.

Outside Carleton's room, they stopped. Loud voices came from inside.

"Look, I don't care," they heard Carleton say. "I think you're way over the line here, and I'm not going to do it."

"You'll do it," a man's voice said, "and you'll do it tomorrow. You're into this thing up to your ears, and it's too late to back down now."

The voices grew lower. Joe and Vanessa leaned close to the door, but now they could hear only muffled talking.

Suddenly, Joe grabbed Vanessa's hand. "Someone's leaving," he whispered. They hurried away from the door and ducked into a stairwell. Joe peered around the corner as the door to Carleton's room opened.

A tall, thin man stepped out of the room, his back toward Joe and Vanessa. They watched him march toward the opposite end of the hall.

"I can't get a look at his face," Joe muttered. "Vanessa, stay here. I'm going to see

60

if I can head him off in front of the building."

Joe dashed out a side door and tore around to the front of the building. He saw the tall man duck into a small green hatchback parked in front of the residence hall.

Joe groaned in frustration. He still hadn't seen the guy's face. He ran back to the side door and tapped on the glass.

Vanessa let him in. "Carleton's leaving his room now," she whispered.

Joe saw Carleton walking to the exit at the far end of the corridor. "Let's check out his room," he whispered.

As soon as Carleton was out of sight, they returned to his room.

"Watch the doors," Joe told Vanessa. He slipped the pick into the lock and began working it. Within seconds the bolt tripped, and they were inside.

Joe closed the door quietly and locked it. They searched the room in a hurry. It was a single, smaller than the Hardys' but with the same basic furniture. The lamp on the end table next to the bed was on.

"This looks interesting," Joe said, pulling a small metal box out of the closet. Inside were a few tools—screwdrivers, pliers, a metal file, and wire cutters.

Joe ran his finger lightly along the paper-thin file. This could be used to cut a pole, he thought. But there was no rust—nothing like the residue he'd seen on the end of Chuck Parrish's broken pole.

He searched the box again and found a wadded-up rag with a few dark smears on it. "Bingo," he said softly. He stuck the rag in his pocket.

Then Joe got another idea. He pulled one of the screwdrivers from the toolbox and picked up the file again. Methodically, he sawed the file back and forth across the handle of the screwdriver.

"What are you doing?" Vanessa asked.

"Filing," Joe said. "If this file was used to cut through Chuck Parrish's vaulting pole, it might leave a pattern on this screwdriver. We can take a look at the pole again and try to match the cut with the one on the screwdriver."

When he was finished, Joe said, "Didn't Carleton tell us during volunteer camp that he went to Northwestern University?" He put the file back in the metal box, stuck the screwdriver in his pocket, and replaced the box in the closet.

"I think so," Vanessa said. "It was one of the Big Ten, I remember that. Why?"

"There's a Utah State windbreaker in here."

"Well, maybe he borrowed it." Vanessa shrugged. "Or somebody gave it to him. I really think you're on the wrong track, Joe. Carleton's okay—just a little pushy."

"Sure, Vanessa, whatever you say," Joe said as he went in to check the bathroom. There was nothing in the medicine cabinet except for shaving stuff and toothpaste. "Let's wrap this up. I don't want to push our luck."

"Hey, what's this?" Vanessa asked. Her voice sounded funny.

Joe joined her at the small desk.

"Look," she said. "This is Carleton's volunteer phone book. And—"

"And look whose name happens to be circled," Joe finished. There were thick red lines around Vanessa's name and around the E-mail address for the broadcasting center. "Looks like he's still after you, Vanessa."

"Maybe he wants a contact in the broadcasting center," she said. "A lot of people want to know what's going on in the Village, and the center is the best source."

In spite of her light tone, Joe knew she was worried. "Look," he began. "You'd better be—"

They both heard the voice in the hall outside the door. "Think so, huh?" Carleton said. His voice grew louder as he came closer. "Well, just wait. The U.S. will take them by thirty points."

Joe saw a look of panic cross Vanessa's face. He gazed around the room for an escape route. Finally, he grabbed her hand and yanked her toward the window just as a key slipped into the door lock.

Chapter

8

THE DOORKNOB TURNED as Joe grabbed the handle on the window. Before he could pop it open, the sound of screeching tires split the night. "Hey, watch out!" someone yelled outside.

Then came a cry from inside the building. "Accident. Hit-and-run!" The cry was echoed by someone else racing down the hall. "Somebody got hit bad!"

Joe and Vanessa froze. They both held their breath as they heard the key click out of the lock. Then Carleton took off down the hall.

"Close call," Vanessa murmured.

Joe held his finger to his lips. He crept over to the door and listened for a second. In the hall, he could hear doors opening and residents spilling out into the corridor.

He motioned Vanessa over, and they slipped out of Carleton's room.

Outside the building was total chaos. A huge crowd had gathered. Joe and Vanessa pushed through and spotted Terry and a teammate kneeling on the ground near a body.

"Oh, no!" Vanessa cried. "Another Cyrenian's been hit!" She grabbed Joe's arm. "It's Coach Masily."

But Joe had noticed something else—a crumpled body lying at the base of a lamppost. "Frank!" Joe rushed over. "Are you okay?"

Joe dropped to the ground next to his brother. Frank still hadn't moved. "Frank! Frank! Can you hear me?" Desperately, Joe looked around for help. "We've got another injury over here!" he yelled. "Help! We need a paramedic."

A big knot had risen on Frank's temple. "It looks like he was knocked out," Vanessa said. "I hope . . ." She didn't finish her thought. Instead, she squeezed Joe's hand and said, "Help's on the way."

A second later Frank's eyes fluttered open. He started to sit up but couldn't make it. "Oh, man," he moaned. "My head."

A wave of relief rushed over Joe. "You look

awful," he said with a grin. "But at least you're conscious."

Frank smiled a little, but Joe could tell that even the small movement hurt. "How about the coach? How is he?" Frank asked.

"We're not sure," Joe said. "Terry and one of the other runners are with him."

"It doesn't look too good," Vanessa said softly.

"That van came out of nowhere, Joe," Frank said. "It was dark blue with a double white pinstripe around the side. The guy driving was stocky, with dark curly hair and a mustache—maybe a small beard, I couldn't see well enough. He was definitely out to nail Coach Masily and me. I didn't catch the license plate."

The emergency crews arrived, and two paramedics came over. One of them checked Frank's vital signs, asked him a few questions, and then tended to his head.

"He's going to be okay," the medic told Joe. "But we'll have to keep him in the hospital overnight for observation. It's a standard precaution with a head injury like this."

Frank closed his eyes again as the crew loaded him onto a stretcher and into the ambulance. Joe went with his brother, promising Vanessa he'd call her later with an update.

As the ambulance pulled away, Joe looked

out the back window. Carleton Fisher had stepped out of the crowd and sidled over to Vanessa.

What does he want from her? Joe wondered. The image of her name circled in the book in Carleton's room came back to him. Joe knew Vanessa could take care of herself, but he was still worried. As soon as he could, he'd check on her.

At the hospital, the paramedics wheeled Frank into the emergency room for a full examination. Coach Masily was already inside, being attended to by two doctors and several nurses.

While Joe waited for the word on Frank, he sat with Detective Posten and Officer Heiser. The two officers were there to question Frank about the accident.

"I thought covering the Olympics would be like a vacation," Officer Heiser said grimly. "Instead, we've been on alert since the opening ceremonies, waiting for the next disaster."

"Have you learned anything more about Chuck Parrish?" Joe asked.

Detective Posten shrugged. "Just that Parrish's pole was the only one damaged."

"There's absolutely no proof that Parrish's pole was deliberately cut," Officer Heiser added. "It was probably just an accidental break. It's not the first time fiberglass has split."

Joe wondered whether the policemen really believed that. He couldn't tell. Still, he knew they couldn't reveal too much to him, so he changed the subject.

"How's the astronaut doing?" Joe asked.

"I heard it was touch-and-go for a while," Heiser said, "but now the word is that he's going to be all right."

Minutes later a nurse beckoned them in. "He's ready to talk."

Frank told the detectives exactly what he'd told Joe about the van. Then the nurse stuck her head in the room. "The patient needs some rest, gentlemen."

The officers arranged to see Frank the next day and said good night. On his way out, Joe grinned at his brother. "Some people will do anything to get out of bunking with me."

Frank waved. "You got that right," he joked.

Before leaving the hospital, Joe called Vanessa. "What was the deal with Carleton?" he asked. "I saw him come over to you after Frank and I left in the ambulance. He didn't hassle you, did he?"

"He asked me out for a soda," Vanessa said. "I told him I was too tired. I still don't think he's dangerous or anything, but he gives me the creeps. Especially after seeing my name circled like that."

"Stay away from him," Joe warned. He told her about Frank, then said good night.

The pole-vault trials finished in the morning, and he had to come back to the hospital to check Frank out. Right now, all he wanted was a good night's sleep.

"Looking good," Joe called out when he arrived at the hospital the next morning. Frank was up, dressed, and already signing out of the hospital.

"I feel pretty good," Frank said. "The doctor says I have to take it easy, but I'm fine. I'll meet you over at the stadium when I'm through with security. They want me to look at some mug shots."

At the Village security office, Frank met with Office Heiser.

"Take your time with the books," the officer said. "We're hoping you'll spot the female driver of the Jeep or the driver of the van that ran you down.

Frank thumbed slowly through the mug shots.

In the locker room at the stadium, Joe cheered. The U.S. coach had just delivered good news. Chuck Parrish had a dislocated shoulder and a broken collarbone, but his doctors expected him to make a full recovery. Parrish was out of this Olympics, but he would be able to compete again in four years. "That's great," Joe told the coach and Parrish's teammates.

The pole-vault trials had finished an hour earlier, and the actual pole-vaulting competition would start in two days. Mr. Hill said the volunteers were off duty until then. Frank joined the other volunteers just as Mr. Hill finished explaining this.

"You're free to go as soon as the clean-up is finished," Mr. Hill said.

"Cool," Joe said. He was looking forward to checking out some of the other Olympic events.

Frank was still moving a little slowly. "Looks like you could use a day or two off," Joe told him as they wheeled two hampers of dirty towels down to the laundry room.

"And let you run this investigation on your own?" Frank joked. "No way."

"Did you recognize any mug shots?" Joe asked.

Frank shook his head in frustration. "I don't think it's a coincidence that Coach Masily and the astronaut are from Cyrena," he said. "And it sounds like the coach knows who launched the attack on the astronaut."

"That's why he was hit," Joe added.

"Exactly," Frank said.

"I still don't get the deal with Chuck Parrish," Joe said. "If the Gurnistanis are responsible for the attacks on Coach Masily and the astronaut, why did they target an American?"

"That's what we've got to find out," Frank said. They began stacking towels in the laundry room. "Our next step—"

"So, Frank," a familiar voice interrupted. "Glad to see you're up and about."

"Thanks, Carleton," Frank mumbled. "How are you feeling?"

Carleton looked at Frank. "What do you mean by that?"

"You didn't show up yesterday afternoon," Frank reminded him. "I thought maybe you were sick."

"Oh, yeah. Bad stomach," Carleton said quickly. "Probably a little food poisoning."

"You heard about Chuck Parrish's accident, I'm sure," Joe said, walking slowly around Carleton. "We were just wondering if you had seen anything suspicious around the locker room before the trials."

Carleton shook his head. "I was sick. I just told you that. What do you think, I'm a liar?"

"I couldn't find you last night, so I drove out to your home address," Joe continued. "You lied about at least one thing, Fisher. Your house was abandoned."

"Okay, okay." Nervously, Carleton turned to watch Joe circling him. "My family moved to Pensacola last year. I gave our old address because I really wanted to volunteer, and I figured local people might get picked first. Give me a break. I just wanted to be a part of this."

Frank kept his eyes on his brother. Carleton sounded sincere, but Joe didn't seem ready to believe him.

"Listen, guys," Carleton said. "We might all get along better if we spent some time together off the job, relaxing. How about starting tonight with dinner at the Rib Shack on Stone Mountain. My treat. Okay?"

Frank and Joe exchanged looks. They'd been meaning to check out Stone Mountain because of the cardboard disk they'd found from the Stonewall Lodge.

"As a matter of fact, we've been wanting to eat there," Frank said. "Sure."

"Great," Carleton said. "You know how to get there?" Frank nodded. "Then let's meet at the Shack at six." Carleton gave them a thumbs-up signal and a smile, then headed off down the stadium tunnel.

"The last thing I want to do is eat with that loser," Joe growled. "I don't trust him."

"Chill, Joe," Frank said. "It's a good chance to find out more about what he's about."

Reluctantly, Joe agreed.

The Hardys finished their chores, then headed for the pole room. Joe wanted another look at Chuck Parrish's severed pole.

Frank took a blank piece of paper and a pencil from his pocket. He held the paper against the severed ends of the two pieces of pole and rubbed the pencil over them, one at a time. Slowly, a diamond pattern appeared on the paper.

Joe did the same with the handle of the screwdriver he had filed with the tool from Carleton's closet. "Check it out!" he exclaimed. The two papers showed the same diamond pattern.

"It's a match," Frank agreed. "Now we know for sure that the pole was cut. A pattern like that wouldn't show up if the pole just snapped."

"And we know who cut it," Joe added. "Our buddy Carleton Fisher."

"Not so fast, Joe," Frank said. "We know that a file like Carleton's probably cut the pole, but that's all. There are plenty of files like the one you found."

"I guess so," Joe muttered. But he was still betting on Carleton as their prime suspect.

The Hardys headed out across the parking lot toward their van. Both were thinking about what their next move should be.

"We've got to find out who the man in Carleton's room was," Joe said.

"Last night, it almost sounded like Carleton was being blackmailed or something. I wonder . . ."

As the two brothers approached the spot where their van was parked, a piercing sound drowned out Joe's next words. It took Joe only a second to recognize the familiar beeping—it was their van's alarm.

Joe saw what had made the alarm go off. It was a hulking figure creeping alongside the van.

Chapter

9

"KIROV!" JOE YELLED. What was Vlad Kirov, the Gurnistani shot-putter, doing near their van?

"I've got him covered, Frank!" Joe yelled. He lunged straight for Kirov's legs.

Joe's tackle was right on target. Kirov went down hard. Joe looked back at the van. The door had been forced open.

Frank heard a grunt from the front of the van. A second massive man approached from the driver's side. And this one held a shiny crowbar in his hand.

The man stepped toward Frank. He raised the crowbar and swung it. Frank ducked, and the tool nicked the side of the van.

"Hey!" Frank yelled. "Watch where you swing that thing!" Out of the corner of his eye, he saw Joe land a karate chop to the front of Kirov's thick neck. The shot-putter fell back, stunned for a moment. Then he came right back at Joe.

The other man stepped toward Frank slowly, ready to swing the crowbar again.

"Joe, I'm not sure we're going to win this one," Frank said. "Let's call it a tie and get out of here."

Joe jumped into the van and crawled over to the driver's seat.

In one quick move, Frank reached down, grabbed a handful of loose gravel, and flung it into the face of the man with the crowbar. Without looking back, he ran around to the passenger side and jumped in.

He held the jimmied door shut as Joe fired up the van, slammed it into reverse, and stood on the accelerator. The van screeched out of the parking lot.

Frank looked back to see the second man hurl the crowbar to the ground. Kirov staggered to his feet.

"Nothing like a little workout to get the heart pumping," Frank said.

"I guess the Gurnistanis don't like us much," Joe said, grinning. "What do you think they were looking for?"

"I don't know. Maybe they weren't looking for anything. Maybe they were just trying to send another warning."

"Or worse," Joe said. "I have a feeling we're on their list of targets."

"Probably." Frank checked the dashboard clock. "Let's pull over, get this door straightened out, and check for any other damage."

Joe drove down a quiet residential street. They circled the block slowly to make sure they weren't being followed, then pulled over. There was nothing missing from the van, and it looked as though the Gurnistanis hadn't had time to find the equipment stowed in the rear compartment.

They used the tire iron to bend the van door back so that the latch would hold as if it were locked. Then they drove to a fast-food restaurant, picked up burgers, fries, and sodas, and headed back to the Village.

In their room Frank unpacked the lunch, and Joe called Vanessa. He listened as she talked, scribbling notes on a scrap of paper. When he hung up, he looked concerned.

"Vanessa had a strange E-mail message on her computer when she got to the broadcasting center this morning," Joe said.

"Who from?"

"Jay Hamilton," Joe said, squeezing mustard on his burger.

"What?"

"You heard me. In the message, he says he got a bum rap when he was thrown off the U.S. pole-vaulting team and sentenced to jail. He said the Olympic Committee and the media really worked him over, and he wants to set the record straight. He asked her to meet him at the fitness exhibit in the lobby of the Crown Hotel tomorrow morning at ten-thirty." Joe stared at Frank. "He told her to come alone."

"But why Vanessa?" Frank asked. "Why did he choose her? She's not even a real reporter."

"I wondered that, too. Vanessa said he claims he doesn't trust the real media people. She figures he got hold of the list of press center volunteers and picked her because her name is at the top of the list. B . . . Bender."

"I don't know," Frank said.

"She's pretty excited," Joe said. "The last line in the message was, 'Don't blow this opportunity. This could make you famous.' "

"We need to figure out a way to guarantee she's safe," Frank said. "Maybe we could wire her and follow somehow."

Joe nodded. "What do you say we head out to Stone Mountain now?" he said. "I'd like to get out there early and look around. Maybe we'll be able to learn more about that cardboard disk we found."

"Sure. We can plan Vanessa's meeting with Jay Hamilton on the way out," Frank agreed.

They changed out of their volunteer outfits and into jeans and polo shirts, then headed down to the lobby. Frank grabbed some schedules and maps from the desk on the way out. Within minutes, Joe had them on the parkway for the sixteen-mile run to the huge granite formation known as Stone Mountain.

"After that encounter in the lot, Kirov and that other thug are at the top of my suspects list," Frank said. "How about you?"

"Absolutely," Joe agreed. "Could one of those guys have been driving the hit-and-run van, too?"

"Kirov and his buddy have blond hair," Frank said. "The van driver had dark hair. So, unless one of them was wearing a wig ..."

"Maybe three guys and a girl are involved. And let's not forget our friend Carleton."

"If Terry is right about Kirov," Frank said, "he's probably not the brains behind this. He and the other guy are probably just hired guns."

"Yeah, but who hired them?" Joe wondered.

"Here's how I see it," Frank said. "When I was looking at mug shots, I got the impression that plenty of people are investigating the crossbow shooting. Because it's the Olympics, the Defense Department is involved, along with Olympic security, the local police, the FBI, and the CIA, too."

"So?" Joe said.

"So, we take on the rest," Frank finished. "We'll keep working on the vaulting sabotage and the hit-and-run." He rubbed his temple. "That one's personal."

"Do you still think they're all connected?"

"That's what we need to figure out," Frank said. "But first we need to figure out how to back up Vanessa for her meeting."

"Right," Joe said.

Frank thumbed through the Olympics brochures and schedules he had brought along. "I thought there was something here about the Crown Hotel." A couple of minutes later, he'd found it. "This is perfect. The Chamber of Commerce is giving an all-day recognition party for Olympic volunteers tomorrow at the Crown Hotel. They're going to have refreshments, entertainment, and, here's the best part, all the volunteers who wore costumes in the opening ceremonies are encouraged to wear them to the party."

"Cool," Joe said. "We can back up Vanessa in costume, and no one will know. We'll just be two more Martians wandering around the hotel."

"Exactly," Frank said as they pulled into Stone Mountain.

" 'The world's largest hunk of exposed granite,' " Frank read from another brochure.

The gray-white granite mountain rose more than eight hundred feet into the sky. Lush green woods and a clear blue lake surrounded it. At the base of the mountain was a recreation area with a plantation village, museums, an old-time railroad, sports and camping facilities, beaches, and wildlife trails. There was also a cable car to ferry tourists to the summit and its spectacular views.

Joe followed the signs to the Stonewall Lodge. "Aha!" He pointed out the big sign with the white-striped triangle on it and then parked the van under it. "We're here."

The lodge consisted of a rustic, one-story main building as well as a circle of tiny one- and two-room cabins scattered under the tall Georgia pines.

"The disk was labeled thirteen," Frank said. "Maybe it's our lucky number." He started toward the main building. "Let's see if we can get somebody to give us some information. Have your volunteer pass ready."

"Good thinking, bro," Joe said. "This town loves us volunteers."

The Hardys walked up to the registration desk. Frank smiled broadly and said to the clerk, "Hi. Would you ring Cabin Thirteen, please, and tell her that her ride is here?"

"Excuse me, sir," the desk clerk said stiffly. He was an older man with a white beard, dressed in jeans and a red-and-black plaid shirt. "Exactly who is the message for?"

"Oh, boy, I was afraid you'd ask that." Frank smiled sheepishly and shook his head. "Look, we're volunteers." He flashed his volunteer card. So did Joe.

The clerk looked at the photos and their faces, then relaxed. "What's up?" he asked.

"This is kind of embarrassing," Frank said, lowering his voice and leaning toward the clerk, "but we're on the transportation team, and we're supposed to pick this lady up and take her downtown. We lost the piece of paper with her name on it. We've been driving so many people around the last few days. All I remember is she's in Cabin Thirteen."

"She's got short hair," Joe chimed in, "something like a buzz cut."

That was all the clerk needed. "Yes, I remember that hair," he said. "Just a moment." He opened a thick notebook and scanned down the lists of names. "Here we are," he said. "It's a Ms. Jane Jordan."

"That's her," Joe said. "Ms. Jordan. Would you call her cabin, please?"

The clerk rang Cabin Thirteen, but there was no answer. Frank thanked him and asked if he wouldn't mind trying again in a few minutes.

The Hardys strolled casually outdoors, then doubled back to the woods behind the main building. They made their way through the trees to Cabin Thirteen.

Frank tapped on the door, and it opened a few inches. "Hello," he called. "Hello?" He pushed the door further with his toe.

The Hardys stepped cautiously inside the one-room cabin. They glanced around quickly. The cabin appeared to be empty.

Frank quickly started searching the room. He checked the desk and bedside table drawers and under the bed. Nothing. Then he opened the closet.

A moment later Frank let out a low whistle. "Check it out, Joe," he said.

Joe hurried over. Lying on the floor of the closet was a crumpled purple Venusian costume. Poking out from under the costume was a jet-black pistol crossbow.

Joe drew in a breath. "Bull's-eye."

Chapter

10

BEFORE THE HARDYS COULD FIGURE out what to do about the weapon lying on the floor, a voice bellowed in their ears, "Put your hands in the air. Now!"

Frank and Joe shot their hands into the air.

"That's good," the voice said. "Now turn around slow, real slow, and keep those hands up."

The Hardys turned to see two men—the Stonewall Lodge desk clerk and a county sheriff. The sheriff frisked them, then emptied their pockets, placing the contents on the dresser. He pulled Joe's volunteer card from his shirt pocket and stared at it.

"Okay now, just what are y'all doing snooping around this nice lady's cabin here?" the sheriff asked. "Looking for something in particular, or just having fun?"

"I'm Frank Hardy, Officer. This is my brother, Joe. We're Olympic volunteers."

"Didn't you say these fellas were in transportation, come to give somebody a ride?" the sheriff asked the clerk.

"That's right." The clerk nodded. "They couldn't remember who."

The sheriff turned back to the Hardys. "Well, this card says Joe works on track-and-field events, not transportation. How about you?" he asked Frank.

"I work in the field events, too, Officer," Frank said. "My card's in my wallet. You can contact Detective Lyle Posten of the Atlanta police or Officer Joe Heiser of Olympic security. They'll vouch for us."

"Oh, really?" the sheriff said. "Well, we're going to take a little ride down to the station house, and you can call them yourself."

The sheriff started poking around the room and stopped at the open closet. "Now, isn't this interesting?" he said, bending down to pick up the pistol crossbow.

"What's going on?" a young woman's voice said. Her accent sounded familiar to Joe. "What are you people doing in my cabin?"

Frank recognized her the minute she stepped

into the room. The last time he'd seen her, she was driving a Jeep, dressed as a Venusian. Tonight, she was in jeans, a white T-shirt, and a black nylon jacket.

"Are you Ms. Jordan?" the sheriff asked.

"I am," the young woman answered, pulling out a passport and handing it to him.

"Well, you had some visitors while you were gone," the sheriff said. "We caught them here."

"These two?" the young woman said. "They are my friends, Frank and Joe Hardy."

Frank nearly choked. He looked at Joe, then at the sheriff and the hotel clerk. They looked as shocked as he felt.

"I've been expecting Frank and Joe," the woman went on. "Now, if you gentlemen will please leave us alone . . ."

"Just a minute, Miss," the sheriff said. "I'm going to have to ask you a few questions. Starting with this." He picked the pistol crossbow up off the dresser where he'd laid it down and held it up to her. "We found it in your closet."

The woman's face went pale. Then she said abruptly, "I have never seen it before. Someone must have put it here."

"The door was open when we came in," Joe said. "Maybe someone was here before us."

"So, you see, this crossbow was planted," the woman said.

"Hold on, everybody," the sheriff said. "I'll do the asking, and you people do the answering. Let's get the story straight here."

The sheriff started with a few routine questions for Jane Jordan, such as where she'd been for the last few hours. She responded with short, clipped answers, checking her watch as if she were in a hurry to end their conversation. She said she'd gone out to see the archery competition two hours earlier.

"I don't know what you're doing with this weapon," the sheriff told her, "but I'm going to let the federal authorities figure it out. Make it easy on yourself, Miss, and stick around." The sheriff handed her his card. "I'm sure you'll be hearing from the Defense Department and the FBI soon—real soon."

The sheriff picked up the crossbow and went out the door. The clerk followed. Jane Jordan immediately shut the door and turned to the Hardys.

"How do you know who we are?" Frank asked.

"My name is Inda Radich," she said. "I talked to Terry Lavrin yesterday. Because you saw me at the opening ceremonies, I have followed you. When I knew you had talked to the Cyrenians several times, I let Terry know I was here.

"He told me about you and that you are

helping to find out who shot our jetpack flier." She began checking around the room, looking in the closet and drawers. "He and Coach Masily think highly of you. I knew when he described you that you were the ones I saw in the parking lot after the crossbow shooting."

"What are you doing here, and why did you register as Jane Jordan?" Frank asked.

"I am a Cyrenian nationalist," she continued. "We are fighting to stay independent of Gurnistan. We are in a battle for our lives. My enemies must never know my identity or whereabouts."

"So why are you identifying yourself to us?" Frank asked. "And why clear us with the sheriff?"

"I had my compatriots check on you." She gave him a slight smile. "We have sources who told us you are to be trusted."

She reached into a small compartment inside her belt and took out two wrinkled photos. "These are the men who have committed the Olympic crimes. They are our enemies from Gurnistan."

"Is that the guy you saw in the hit-and-run van?" Joe asked Frank. "The one with the beard?"

Frank took one look and said, "That's him."

"He is Gregor Stefanov," Inda Radich said, "a crossbow master."

"Do you think he's the one who planted the crossbow here?"

"Of course he did," she said briskly. "He wants me to be accused of assaulting the jetpacker."

"How did he know someone else would find it?" Frank asked. "There was a good chance you'd be the one to discover it. You could have tossed it, or turned it in to the authorities."

She shrugged. "I don't have the answer to your question. Maybe Stefanov was more concerned with sending a message to me than framing me for his crime."

"What were you doing at the opening ceremonies?" Joe asked.

"I was shadowing Stefanov and his fellow assassin, Ivan Kalery. I stole a costume as a disguise. But I failed to prevent the attack." She looked down at her feet and shook her head. "I saw the Gurnistanis go down the ropes. I went after them, but you distracted me with your chase, and I lost them."

"I still don't understand why the Gurnistanis picked the Olympics to launch a terrorist attack," Joe said. "They must know they won't get away with it."

"Oh, but they believe they will," she said. "The whole world is watching, and they are thumbing their noses, saying they can do anything they want and no one can stop them."

"They're wrong this time," Frank said. "They won't get away with this." He looked over at his brother and could tell Joe was thinking the same thing. He was also probably wondering if Inda Radich was telling the truth.

She sighed. "Now I must move," she said. "They will be back for me." She spoke matter-of-factly. There was no fear in her voice, only disgust.

"How about Kirov?" Joe asked. "We had a run-in with him and a friend. Are they in on it, too?"

"Probably," she answered, "but just as hired thugs. If Gurnistan was defeated, they would be the first to defect. Kirov is more interested in his fame as a shot-putter than his allegiance to his country."

"Look, Ms. Radich," Frank began. "We can help you track these guys down. Any idea where the Gurnistanis are staying?"

"I don't know yet," she said. "Somewhere here on the mountain. I have followed them several times but lost them every time." She put the photos away. "Thank you for your offer of help, but I will handle the investigation myself. I know my enemies and what they can do. I do not need help from amateurs, even talented ones such as yourselves."

"Have you talked to any of the authorities

about this—the FBI, the Defense Department?" Frank asked.

"They will soon be calling me because of the weapon," she said. "But this is an internal matter between my people and the administration of Gurnistan. We have asked the world for help many times in the past but are told our problems are too insignificant. We have learned that we must deal with them ourselves."

"Where exactly have you lost track of these guys before?" Frank asked.

"Twice at the Olympic archery site and once near the campground," she said. She stood and gave them a tight smile. "If you will please go now, I have much work to do."

The Hardys tried asking a few more questions, but Inda Radich had finished talking. "This is my investigation," was all she'd say. "Stay out of it. You are rooming at the Village, are you not? If I need further help, I shall contact you there." Reluctantly, the Hardys left. She bolted her cabin door behind them.

"I don't know," Joe said as they walked to the van. "I don't quite trust her. For one thing, I didn't like that 'amateur' crack. If she's here alone, she should have jumped at our offer to help."

"Maybe she's not alone," Frank said. "We can call Terry and check on her story when we get back to the Village." He checked his watch. "We've got a couple of hours before we meet Carleton. Inda Radich said she saw the Gurnistanis near the archery center and the campground. Let's check them out."

"What about the crossbow?" Joe said. "What if it's hers? Maybe she's just posing as a Cyrenian."

"We can't rule that out," Frank said. "Although if that were the case, she probably would have let the sheriff haul us off." When they reached the van, he said, "Okay, let's split up. I'll take the shuttle to the campground. I can walk to the Rib Shack from there. You go check out the archery center, then meet me at the Shack just before six."

Joe followed Stonewall Jackson Drive along the lakeshore to the archery center. The range was large, about the size of a soccer field. The greensward was freshly cut and trimmed. Brightly colored targets lined one side.

The event was already under way. Most spectators sat on white bleachers. VIPs and the press occupied a small, air-conditioned building at one end of the range. Behind it, a five-story bell tower rose above the lakeshore.

Joe stopped to watch one of the archers pull his fifty-five-pound bowstring back in a full draw. The arrow streaked at more than one hundred miles per hour to the target, a bull's-eye the size of a silver dollar seventy meters away.

Pulling his visor down to shield his eyes from the sun, Joe scanned the grounds once more. If Inda Radich was telling the truth, the Gurnistanis had been hanging around here.

His volunteer card allowed him more access than an ordinary spectator. He walked behind the bleachers, searching the ground and inspecting the scaffolding. He was looking for something—anything—that might draw the Gurnistanis here. He hated to think about it, but the Gurnistanis could be planning another attack. Would they choose the archery center as their next site?

He ambled over to where the competitors were assembled, then strolled around the VIP building as far as he could before the security officer turned him back.

Joe scanned the area again. What would I do if I were going to cause a little trouble? he thought. His gaze rested on the bell tower at the edge of the lake.

He walked quickly to the base of the five-story structure. A park ranger's pickup truck was parked in the woods behind the tower, but there was no sign of anyone nearby. The front door was padlocked, and the only windows were at the top.

Joe walked around to the back and found a

narrow maintenance door. The small padlock on its latch had been smashed and was lying on the ground. He stepped inside, being careful to move quietly. The tower was a hollow cylinder with a small elevator. A metal staircase also led upward.

Joe started up the winding staircase. Halfway up, he stopped to take off his sneakers. He'd make a lot less noise now.

Joe continued up the staircase. A half-dozen steps from the top, he stopped again. He could hear rustling sounds and grunting. Somebody up there was doing something. And whatever he was doing, he was in a hurry.

Joe inched his way up the staircase until he could see into the top floor.

It was a tall circular space with several clusters of bells hanging from the ceiling. Large, open windows circled the room.

In front of Joe was a figure dressed in a black jumpsuit. Even from the back, Joe could tell it was Vlad Kirov who was kneeling over a cylindrical object that lay on the floor.

Joe's heart stopped when he realized what it was: a rocket-propelled grenade launcher.

Chapter

11

JOE FLEW BACK DOWN THE STAIRS. It looked as if Vlad Kirov was still assembling the launcher, which meant Joe had a little time—very little time—to stop the Gurnistani terrorist from his next destructive act.

Come now, Joe told himself. He's bigger and stronger, but you're a lot smarter. You can come up with something.

He threw open the door next to the elevator. It was a maintenance closet. He spotted a large push broom and pulled it out. Then he hit the elevator button.

The elevator door whooshed open. Joe jumped inside, then used the end of the broom to pop out the panel on the ceiling of the car.

Joe pushed the broom end up into the opening and hooked it onto the roof of the elevator so that the handle hung down. He jumped up and hoisted himself through the opening until he was crouched on the roof of the elevator.

Joe looked up. The elevator's cables reached nearly to the top of the bell tower. He could see that the elevator made one stop, at the floor Kirov was on. If he was right, he could crouch on the roof of the elevator car all the way to the top. It looked as if there was plenty of room above his head.

Joe glanced back at the three buttons on the panel beside the door: Up, Down, and Alarm. He grabbed the broom and pressed up with the tip.

The elevator bounced as it began its slow glide upward. Joe tried not to think about how much—or how little—time was left. Instead, he concentrated on making his plan work.

The elevator reached the top floor, and the door slid open. Joe stayed in position on top of the elevator, poised for action. His heart beat double-time.

Kirov heard the elevator and made a guttural sound. He threw down a tool and got to his feet. Joe listened to him approach the elevator and tightened his grip on the broom.

Kirov stepped inside the car, a revolver in his

hand. With a powerful motion, Joe slammed the push broom, bristles first, into Kirov's face.

Kirov screamed in surprise. As his hands flew up to his eyes, the gun dropped to the floor and slid to the corner of the elevator. Joe jammed the broom down again—into the back of Kirov's neck. The huge shot-putter fell forward with a grunt.

Joe dropped through the opening and onto Kirov's back. Then he made a leap for the gun lying on the floor.

Kirov started to struggle to his feet, but the sight of the gun in Joe's hand stopped him cold. Keeping the gun trained on the Gurnistani, Joe pushed the Down button, then hit Alarm.

Minutes after the elevator reached the bottom of the tower, a maintenance man and an Olympic security officer arrived. "What's going on?" the security man said. He stared at the gun.

Joe introduced himself and told the men about the grenade launcher. The security man quickly handcuffed Kirov to the stairway railing.

"How did you get in?" he asked Joe. "And exactly what were you doing in the first place?"

"I entered the back door," Joe answered. "I had a feeling something was going on over here in the tower, and I followed my hunch. It's kind of a long story. Do you know Officer Heiser?" Joe asked.

The security man nodded.

"You can call him," Joe said. "He'll vouch for me."

The security man called Officer Heiser on his two-way radio. The conversation was brief.

"Okay," the officer said when he clicked off. "So who's this guy?"

"He's a shot-putter from Gurnistan," Joe said. "I've had a few run-ins with him before."

Six more vehicles pulled up outside the bell tower. Officers in plain clothes and in uniforms swarmed toward the scene. Joe led them to the launcher on the top floor and told them about Kirov and his friend breaking into the van in the stadium parking lot. Then he glanced at his watch. He was late for dinner with Carleton and Frank. At least I have a good excuse, he thought.

"I assume Officer Heiser knows where to reach you," the security officer said. Joe nodded, and the officer said, "All right, go ahead. We'll be in touch."

Joe hurried back to the van. He sped over to the Rib Shack near the campground. Frank and Carleton were already there. As soon as Carleton got up to use the rest room, Joe told Frank about the close call with Kirov.

"A grenade launcher?" Frank's eyes went wide.

"It was unbelievable," Joe said. "He was probably planning to fire that baby right into the crowd."

"Nice going, Joe," Frank said. "Maybe the security guys can get Kirov to cough up some information."

"Don't say anything to Carleton about this," Joe cautioned. "Let's see what we can get out of him tonight."

Frank nodded.

Carleton came back, and they ordered dinner. The southerner kept up a steady flow of conversation about the games and about being volunteers. Joe forced himself to act polite.

Gradually, Joe steered the conversation around to the shooting incident at the opening ceremonies. "Carleton, weren't you sitting up on the back of the stands with some other guys?" he asked.

"Yeah, there were a bunch of us up there."

"Do you know who any of those other guys were?" Joe continued.

Carleton grinned. "Yeah. Martians, Neptunians, Venusians."

Frank smiled politely. "You didn't know who any of the aliens were under the costumes?"

Carleton shook his head. "Nope."

"And you're sure you didn't see anything funny go on?" Joe asked.

"Not at all," Carleton said. "Why do you guys keep asking me this?"

"It's just so amazing that you were up there at the time of the attack. I mean, you were right with the action," Frank said.

"Better view up there, y'all." Carleton shrugged. "And I don't mean of the astronaut. Did you catch those women on the field, the ones with the torchbearer? That's what I was watching."

Frank and Joe exchanged looks. Was Carleton telling the truth? For the rest of their meal, Carleton went on about all the great-looking girls he'd seen since the games began.

Joe kept thinking about Vanessa and her name being circled in the book in Carleton's room. Why? Maybe he'd just been planning to ask her out.

When the Hardys finally arrived back at their room in the Village, there was a message from Officer Heiser. Frank returned the call.

"Kirov denies everything," Frank said after he hung up. "He says the back door of the bell tower was unlocked, so he wandered in and went to the top for a better view of the archery. He says he found the rocket launcher there and pushed the elevator alarm to call security. He didn't want to walk out of there with it because he thought it would scare people."

"Did the police question him about breaking into our van?" Joe said.

"Kirov says they were just walking through the parking lot and heard the alarm. They rushed over to investigate and saw the jimmied door."

"Right," Joe muttered. "So why'd they come after us with a crowbar?"

"He says they didn't know we were the owners," Frank said. "He thought we might be the guys who broke in."

"Heiser doesn't buy that," Joe said. "Does he?"

"I don't think so, but I guess there's not enough evidence to hold Kirov. By the way, Kirov says he's going to sue you for assault. And Officer Heiser made a crack about us really getting around. He heard from the Stone Mountain sheriff, too."

Joe laughed as Frank dialed Terry's room. "I guess we *do* get around."

When Terry answered, Frank told him briefly about their meeting with Inda Radich.

"It doesn't surprise me that she doesn't want your help. She seems independent and headstrong," Terry said.

"Any chance she's working for the other side?" Frank asked.

"I think she is loyal to our cause," Terry said, "but I do not know her well personally. War changes people. Nothing would surprise me anymore."

Frank said goodbye to Terry, handed the phone to Joe, and headed for the shower. "Tell Vanessa to be here at nine tomorrow," he said over his shoulder. "Two aliens will be accompanying her to the Crown Hotel."

"I'm sure she'll be thrilled," Joe replied with a grin.

Vanessa showed up right on time, wearing white jeans and a volunteer's green polo shirt and white cap. The Hardys had gotten hold of their alien costumes and put them on again.

"You sure you're okay with this, Vanessa?" Joe asked. "You're not scared of this guy?"

"Absolutely not," Vanessa said. "Hey, I'm a member of the media now. How could I pass up an exclusive interview with Jay Hamilton? It's really exciting."

"It could be exciting, all right," Frank said. "It could also be a trap. You know his reputation."

"At least we get a chance to try this out." Joe pulled out a miniature electronic transmitter and receiver set their father had given them.

"Cool," Vanessa said. "That's what I'll be wearing—that tiny thing?"

Joe nodded. The wireless bug was the size of a small button. "Dad says it works great." Joe clamped it to the back of Vanessa's sunburst necklace.

"Joe, I'll wear the receiver," Frank said. "You keep track of Vanessa by sight." Joe handed the device to Frank, who put it in his ear. It would be totally hidden under his Martian mask.

"Okay," Joe said. "Let's give it a try."

Vanessa tested the microphone by walking out to the parking lot ahead of Frank and Joe. She talked as she went down the hall and deliberately opened and closed the door to the building. When she got outside, she said, "If you can hear me, come on out." Frank gave Joe a thumbs up. He'd heard everything.

The Hardys caught up with Vanessa, and they all got into the van.

"It's show time," Joe said.

At the Crown Hotel downtown, they dropped Vanessa near the front entrance. She was due to meet Jay Hamilton at ten-thirty at the fitness exhibit in the lobby.

The Hardys parked the van in the garage downstairs and followed a group of tourists into the hotel.

The lobby was huge, with an atrium rising

fifteen stories. Sunlight poured down through a skylighted roof. Joe could see Vanessa's blond hair ahead in the crowd. She was walking toward a fitness display. Frank concentrated on the sounds in his ear. There was so much traffic and activity around them—he'd better stay focused.

"Vanessa!" Frank suddenly heard a man's voice.

"Hello." Vanessa sounded friendly but a little nervous. "Are you Jay Hamilton?"

"Walk straight ahead," the man said gruffly.

"Where are we going?" Vanessa replied.

"Just shut up and do as I say."

"Vanessa's in trouble," Frank said, pressing the receiver closer into his ear.

The Hardys rushed straight over to the fitness exhibit. It was crowded with exercise clothing and people trying out equipment. But Vanessa was nowhere in sight.

"I can't believe we lost her," Joe moaned.

Frank held up his hand for Joe to be quiet. He could barely hear the receiver over the buzz of the crowd. Finally, he heard a familiar sound. "I got it!" he said.

"What is it?" Joe said.

"It's an elevator. I heard the doors close and a bell dinging."

Frank and Joe looked up to search around the atrium for the elevators. There was a bank of glass ones that soared up the middle of one wall.

Vanessa stood in one as it rose from the floor, her eyes wide with fear. There was only one other figure in the elevator—a tall, thin Neptunian who stood up against Vanessa's back, holding his body unnaturally close to her.

Chapter

12

JOE TOOK OFF IN A FLASH. He zigzagged through the crowd, reaching the elevator bank at the far end of the atrium in less than ten seconds.

Frank ran after him, pressing the receiver tightly to his ear. "Where are we going?" he heard Vanessa ask. There was no answer. A few seconds later, she said, "I demand to know where you're taking me." No answer again.

The Hardys jumped into the first available elevator.

"Hold it, Joe," Frank said as he reached to push the button for the top floor. "She just said something about 'out on the roof.'"

"Good girl," Joe said quietly. He tapped his

foot impatiently as the doors slowly closed. "Come on, let's move it!"

Frank peeled off his mask and stuffed it into his billowy costume shirt. Joe followed suit, and seconds later, the elevator let out a ding as they reached the top floor.

Frank and Joe located the exit door at the end of the hall and raced toward it. They bounded up the short staircase to the roof. Cautiously, they cracked open the door and looked outside.

Vanessa sat on a cement block about twenty yards away. Standing over her was the Neptunian, his back to the door.

The Hardys crept out onto the roof and slipped behind a large air-conditioning unit. Joe couldn't hear what the man was saying. Frank listened carefully to the device in his ear.

"I want to know more about your friends, Vanessa," the Neptunian said. Frank's heartbeat quickened. "They've been snooping around about Parrish's pole-vaulting accident. I need to know what they've found out."

"I don't know what you're talking about," Vanessa said. "What friends?"

"You know who I mean," he said. "Your boyfriends from home."

"How do you know so much about me?"

Vanessa asked. "Have we met somewhere before?"

"Just answer my question."

"No," Vanessa snapped back. "Not until you take off that mask so I can see you."

"Listen, I'm getting tired of this. Don't try to play Little Miss Reporter with me. Just answer my questions, and nobody gets hurt."

Joe watched Vanessa cross her arms and stick out her chin in defiance. This time, he could hear her say, "No answers until you take a step back and pull off your mask."

Joe turned to Frank to find out what the man said next.

Suddenly, Frank frowned.

Before Joe could figure out what was happening, Vanessa screamed Joe's name. The Hardys raced across the roof. The Neptunian was standing over her, holding a large hunting knife.

Joe hurled himself at the man, and they both tumbled back toward the wall. With one powerful chop, Joe hacked the knife out of the man's hand.

Vanessa jumped out of the way as Frank dove for the knife. The man lunged at Joe, butting him with the bald, swollen head of the Neptunian mask.

Joe groaned and slumped over. Frank started for the man, but Joe struggled to his feet. Pushing past his brother, he delivered a short, powerful blow to the man's chin with the heel of his right hand.

The man reeled, then staggered backward into litter strewn across the roof. Joe pressed his advantage, moving toward the guy. But the Neptunian was quick. He reached behind him and grabbed something, which banged against the roof with a crash. Then he whipped his arm back around. In his hand was a broken bottle, its jagged edges aimed right at Joe's head.

Joe ducked, and the man staggered forward. He regained his balance and lunged toward Vanessa. He grabbed her and wheeled her around, holding the broken bottle against her cheek.

"Let her go!" Joe shouted.

Without saying a word, the Neptunian backed over to the door. He reached behind him for the knob. Then he shoved Vanessa down hard, opened the door, and disappeared into the hotel.

"I'll go after him," Frank said. "You check Vanessa."

Frank tore across the roof and through the door. He could hear someone running down the stairs a few floors below. He raced down five flights, steadily gaining on the alien from Neptune.

At the landing, the man stopped and looked back for a split second. Frank froze as the Neptunian's weird, bulging eyes fixed on him. Abruptly, the man spun around and bolted through the door onto the tenth floor.

In the hall, people were streaming out of a conference room. Frank sprinted after Vanessa's captor, dodging curious onlookers who stared in amazement at the two aliens running by.

"Coming through!" he yelled. A large woman in a flowered dress panicked and stepped into Frank's path. He managed to avoid knocking her over, but when he looked up, he realized he had lost the Neptunian. He had disappeared.

Finally, Frank stopped to catch his breath. He asked several people, but no one had seen where the Neptunian went. Frank went back to the stairs and started toward the roof. Several floors up, he met Joe and Vanessa coming down.

"I lost him," Frank said. "Was it Jay Hamilton?" he asked Vanessa.

"I don't know," she said as they went into the eleventh floor hallway to wait for an elevator.

"Let's check in at the fitness exhibit," Joe said. "If it wasn't Hamilton, he may still be there waiting for you."

They scanned the lobby but saw no sign of a man waiting for Vanessa.

"How about the desk?" Joe suggested. "Maybe he left a message."

Vanessa went over and asked the clerk if Mr. Hamilton had left a message for her.

"Yes, here you are." The clerk handed her a yellow slip of paper.

"It's from Jay Hamilton." Vanessa read the note. "He says he can't meet with me today, that an emergency came up. He says he'll call later tonight or tomorrow morning and reschedule."

Frank went back to the desk. "Could you call Mr. Jay Hamilton's room, please?"

"Certainly," the desk clerk said. He called up the guest roster on his monitor and said, "I'm sorry, but Mr. Hamilton checked out last night."

"Any forwarding information?" Frank asked.

"No, sir, I'm sorry, there isn't."

"Well, we know for sure he's been in town," Joe said. "At least, until last night."

"He definitely knows his way around a track-and-field stadium," Frank pointed out. "And he knows pole vaulting. He could have bluffed his way into the locker rooms and cut Chuck Parrish's pole."

"I thought you suspected the Gurnistanis—or Carleton," Vanessa said.

"Hamilton has a stronger motive," Joe admitted. "He was thrown off the team, jailed, his reputation ruined."

"But why would he shoot the jetpacker? Or run down Coach Masily?" Frank asked.

"Maybe they're not connected." Joe was thinking out loud. "Maybe it's different people doing two different things—the Gurnistanis attacking the Cyrenians and Hamilton getting back at the U.S. team."

Frank nodded. "That's a definite possibility."

"So what next?" Vanessa asked.

"First we get out of these costumes," Frank said. The three went through the lobby and to the stairs that led to the underground parking lot.

The Hardys got into the van and stowed the electronic bug in the special compartment. Then they peeled off their costumes. They were wearing jeans and T-shirts underneath. Suddenly, Vanessa pointed out the window. "Joe! Frank! It's him!"

Joe slid the door open.

"Look, there he goes," Vanessa said. "The Neptunian. Same tall guy, same walk. I'm sure it's him." The Hardys watched the man get into a green hatchback.

"That car looks familiar, too," Joe said.

"Remember the guy who was shouting at Carleton? That guy drove the same car."

"So let's go." Frank started the van.

As usual, the downtown area was jammed. Frank tried to keep an eye on the hatchback as it wove its way through traffic.

"There he is," Joe said. The car turned into a car rental agency. They watched the man pull off his mask, revealing dark hair. He strode quickly into the office. "I still can't get a good look at his face," Joe mumbled.

Frank eased the van into a parking place across the street. They idled there, waiting for the Neptunian to come out. They could see him inside the building. It looked as if he was returning the car and paying his bill.

They watched the man go into a room at the side of the car rental office. A few minutes passed, then a tall, thin man wearing a brown warmup suit came out of the building. His face was shielded by large sunglasses and a cap with the visor pulled low.

"He ditched the costume," Frank said.

The man walked across the street and started down a set of wide steps leading to a wall of glass doors. Olympic banners fluttered from poles, and banks of colorful flowers lined the steps. "What's that?" Joe said. "Where's he going?"

"The Underground," Frank said, checking his map.

"Let's go get him," Joe said.

The Underground was a major tourist attraction. Set below modern ground level, it contained a section of the original city of Atlanta. Pre–Civil War buildings had been restored and turned into shops, clubs, and restaurants. Authentic old street lamps lit the wide promenades. The sounds of rock and jazz music floated out from clubs and across the mall.

"Let's split up," Frank said. He gestured to the left. "You guys go that way; I'll go right."

Frank watched Joe and Vanessa take off, then turned in the opposite direction. He leaped down a short staircase and took a ramp down to the next level. He wound his way deeper and deeper into the bustling Underground.

He stopped in at every shop and club, took a quick look around, and moved on. He finally turned a corner and came to a dead end. The promenade widened and stopped at a long iron railing. Beyond the railing was a three-story drop to the narrow alley at the bottom of the Underground.

Frank scanned the scene. Across the alley was a three-story bank of restaurants and clubs, each with its own balcony full of tables.

There were hundreds of people, but he couldn't pick out a tall man in a brown warmup suit.

Just as he was about to turn and continue his search, Frank heard footsteps behind him. Then he felt two strong hands grab the back of his shirt and shove him hard.

Frank was pinned tight against the railing. He struggled to break free, but his attacker leaned his entire weight into him. Frank could feel the iron railing grinding into his stomach. He was trapped.

Then Frank felt the man's hands grip his legs. A second later his feet flew into the air and toppled over the railing.

The air rushed out of his lungs as he fell over the edge into thin air.

Chapter

13

THE LAST THING FRANK SAW was people on the balconies across the alley pointing as they watched him go over the railing. A woman below screamed in horror.

Desperately, Frank reached back for the railing. His fingers grazed the iron spindles but couldn't grip them. Then his outstretched fingers caught something else.

It was an Olympic banner, about eight feet long, white with five colored connecting rings. The banner hung from the bottom of the railing.

Frank clung with all his might to the cloth. He dangled three stories over the narrow alley below. His heart pumped furiously. If he fell, it was over for sure.

Carefully, Frank released one hand and quickly clutched a fistful of material higher up the banner. Slowly, he repeated the move with the other hand, trying not to think about what would happen if the cloth ripped. Hand over hand, he climbed up the banner.

Finally, he reached the bottom of the railing. He grabbed onto the iron spindles, then swung his legs up until his heels caught the bottom of the railing. With one more mighty heave, he hoisted his body up over the railing. A few people from the crowd reached out to give him a hand.

Cheers and whistles erupted from the hundreds of spectators on the balconies across the way and in the alley below. "You a gymnast?" one man called. Frank shook his head, then thanked the people who'd helped him. Adrenaline was still rushing through his body.

"Frank!" Joe raced toward him.

"Just in time to help, as usual," Frank remarked. "I'm okay."

"We heard that someone fell over a railing and was hanging three stories up," Joe said. "I figured it was either you or that other guy. What happened?"

"I didn't exactly fall," Frank said, flexing his back. "The other guy—"

"Pushed you?" Vanessa finished.

Frank nodded. "I'm pretty sure it was our friend in the green car."

"I saw exactly what happened," a man from the crowd said. "The guy shoved me out of the way and sent me flying. Then he pinned you up against the rail and pushed you over."

"What did he look like?" Joe asked.

"Tall and thin," the man said. "He was wearing a brown jogging suit. I've never seen anything like it. It was as if that guy wanted to kill you!"

"You didn't see where he went, did you?" Frank asked.

The man shook his head.

"Thanks for your help," he said. He turned to Joe and Vanessa.

"Let's get out of here. I've had enough of the Underground."

They walked back to the van, got in, and drove to the car rental agency. In the trash can in the men's room, they found the blue costume. The rental agent told them the car was leased to a Joseph Johnson but refused to give out any more information.

Frank put in a call to Olympic security and left a message for Officer Heiser to call him. He wanted to report what had happened to Vanessa.

Their next stop was for lunch at a crowded diner.

"Well, we know that whoever grabbed me was trying to sabotage the pole vaulting," Vanessa said, taking a bite of her tuna salad sandwich.

"That was the only incident the guy mentioned, right?" Frank said. "He didn't say anything about the astronaut or the hit-and-run on Coach Masily?"

Vanessa nodded.

"We've got to figure out whether it was Jay Hamilton who grabbed you," Joe said.

"Vanessa, maybe you could check the database on him," Frank said. "Get the full scoop. Background, physical description, everything."

"Sure." Vanessa nodded.

"I'd like to go over to the stadium and talk to the vaulters again," Joe said. "Maybe there's been another Jay Hamilton sighting."

"Okay, it's two-thirty now," Frank said. "I'll go check on Coach Masily at the hospital, see if he's well enough to talk. Maybe he can tell me the names he was about to give before he got hit."

The Hardys walked Vanessa to the train station. Joe told her he'd be taking the cellular phone from the van with him. She promised to give him a call as soon as she had the information on Hamilton.

Vanessa jumped on a train for the broadcasting center, and the Hardys headed out in the van. Joe dropped off Frank at the hospital.

"See you later," Frank called. "I'll catch up with you at the stadium."

At the hospital Frank was glad to find Coach Masily sitting up in bed and eating. Terry Lavrin was there, helping him.

"How are you doing?" Frank asked the coach.

He started to reply in English, then gave up. Finally, he answered in Cyrenian, with Terry translating.

"He is doing much better," Terry said. "He has a few broken ribs, a collapsed lung, and a concussion, but he will be okay."

The coach spoke again. "He asks how is his comrade in disaster?" Terry said.

"Fine," Frank said, pulling his hair back. "See? Just a bruise. I'm happy you're doing well."

The coach smiled and nodded.

"Coach Masily, that night you said you know who shot the jetpack flier," Frank said.

The coach rattled off a flurry of Cyrenian. Terry calmed him, then turned to Frank. "He is having memory problems since the accident. The doctors are hopeful his memory will return."

"He didn't confide in you that night?" Frank asked.

Terry shook his head. "No. This is the first I am hearing of this."

On a hunch Frank threw out the names Inda Radich had given them—the two men she claimed were behind the attacks.

"Ask him if the names Stefanov and Kalery mean anything to him," Frank urged.

Terry spoke to the coach, and the coach hesitated for a moment. Then he shook his head sadly.

"If he can't remember their names, maybe he can remember what they look like," Frank said. "Maybe he could draw a rough sketch or talk to a police artist."

The coach was very agitated and answered in Cyrenian.

"He can't remember anything about them," Terry said. "His injuries have made him confused."

The coach fell back on his pillow.

"He is tired," Terry said. "Perhaps you can return later."

Frank apologized for disturbing them, then left and walked to the stadium. He found Joe and told him about his visit with Coach Masily.

"I've talked to quite a few pole vaulters," Joe said. "No one saw anything or anyone suspicious hanging around the equipment room."

"Which confirms it had to be someone with access," Frank said. "Someone who wouldn't arouse suspicions."

"Maybe it's time to check Carleton Fisher's locker," Joe said.

Frank agreed, and they headed for the volunteer locker room. Suddenly, the cellular phone buzzed from Joe's duffel bag. Joe answered, listened, and said, "Okay."

"It was Vanessa," he told Frank after he hung up. "She's got something important but doesn't want it going out over the airwaves. I'm calling her back on the pay phone in the hall. Be right back."

He returned in ten minutes. "Frank, this is good stuff," he said. "Vanessa found photos of Jay Hamilton. He's the same height and build as the guy who dragged her to the roof."

"But none of us has seen that guy's face yet," Frank reminded him. "Height and build may match, but—"

"Wait, there's more," Joe said. "Guess where Jay Hamilton went to college."

Before Frank could answer, he went on: "Utah State. Carleton had a Utah State jacket in his closet, remember? You said the person who sabotaged Chuck Parrish had to be someone with access and someone who knew about pole vaulting. I think you were right both times. Carleton has the inside track, and Jay Hamilton has the vaulting know-how."

"I believe we were about to check Mr. Fisher's locker when the phone rang," Frank replied.

Joe nodded. "Absolutely."

While Frank stood guard, Joe pulled a screwdriver from his duffel bag and used it to jimmy the locker door open.

Then Frank heard footsteps approaching. Someone was coming toward the locker room. He signaled to Joe, who closed the locker door quietly. Frank peered out of the room. "Believe it or not, it's the man himself," he said. "Carleton."

"I'll hold him," Joe whispered. "Maybe you'd better try Officer Heiser and Detective Posten again. Tell them our theory about Fisher and Hamilton."

Frank nodded and hurried away. Joe heard Carleton greet Frank and then come into the locker room. His back was to Joe.

"Carleton," Joe said in a loud voice. "I'm surprised to see you."

Carleton jumped, slamming the locker door. "Joe Hardy! What are you doing here?"

"Chuck Parrish asked me to pick up his poles for him," Joe explained. "Since he's obviously not going to be using them for a while."

"Right. It's a real shame," Carleton said. "Well, I'm out of here. See you tomorrow for the real action. Pole vaulting starts in the morning." As he headed toward the door, Joe noticed his right arm was tucked behind his back.

"What's your hurry, Carleton?" Joe asked. He stepped between Carleton and the door. "Stick around a while longer. I have some ideas about what's been going on, and I'd like to run them by you."

Carleton's eyes narrowed as he studied Joe. "So what are your ideas?" he demanded.

"Frank and I have done some checking, and it seems that Chuck Parrish's pole didn't just snap in two. It was sliced, probably with a rusty file."

Carleton's eyes shifted briefly, but he didn't say anything.

"I saw you in a Utah State jacket once," Joe lied. "Isn't that where Jay Hamilton went? Did you know him? Is he the hothead the papers all say he is?"

"I don't know what you're talking about," Carleton said. "But I'm outta here."

"Not until you've talked to security about your rusty file and the vaulting poles and your connection to Jay Hamilton."

"That's enough, Hardy," Carleton said. Sweat beaded on his temple as he whipped his hand around. He pointed a gun at Joe. "Now move out of the way. I'm not afraid to use this."

Joe looked at the gun and laughed out loud. "Give it up, Fisher. That's a starter pistol. It shoots blanks."

"Really?" Carleton sneered. He took aim at the wall just to the side of Joe's head and squeezed the trigger. A deafening bang echoed through the locker room.

Joe turned to see a bullet hole in the wall behind him.

Chapter

14

THE STARTER PISTOL wasn't shooting blanks.

"For the last time, move out of my way!" This time, Carleton aimed the pistol directly at Joe's face.

Joe raised his arms in the air and stepped toward him. "Now, just a minute, Carleton," he said slowly.

Carleton opened his mouth to reply, but before any words came out, Joe dove for Carleton's legs. It was a good tackle. Carleton fell back, his arms flew up in the air, and the gun fired again into the ceiling.

Joe banged Carleton's wrist against the floor, popping the gun out of his hand. It slid toward the wall. As Joe pinned Carleton's shoulders to the floor, Frank ran into the room.

Frank scooped up the gun and examined it. "It looks like a thirty-eight starter pistol," he said. "What's Carleton doing with this?"

"Trying to talk me into letting him leave," Joe said. "Careful with that. It's loaded with live ammo."

While Frank held the pistol, Joe stood up. Carleton stayed put.

Joe went over to check out the gun. He'd learned a little about starters from his track coach at Bayport High. At most local events, like a high school meet, a regular starter pistol, a twenty-two with a sealed barrel, and wax or clay blank wads were used. At bigger events—college track meets, championships, the Olympics—a thirty-eight might be fired. The louder bang added to the anticipation and excitement of the event.

Both Frank and Joe knew that if you didn't seal off the barrel of a starter, it could work just like the real thing.

"Security's on the way," Frank said. He clicked open the chamber of the gun and dropped the remaining four slugs into his hand. "Looks like you've been doing a little work on this one, Carleton. Once the police get here, you'll have some explaining to do."

Carleton shook his head. Right now, he wasn't saying a word.

A few minutes later Officer Heiser and Detective Posten arrived. Joe filled them in. The officers read Carleton his rights, then asked him about Jay Hamilton. When Carleton stayed silent, Detective Posten said, "We probably have enough evidence to convict you. Full cooperation might earn you a lighter sentence."

"It was all Hamilton's idea," Carleton mumbled. Now he was ready to talk.

"What was Hamilton's idea?" the detective asked.

"Sabotaging Parrish's pole. Hamilton wanted revenge on the American team and the Olympic Committee for his disqualification. He paid me to help him out."

"How much?" Joe asked.

"Ten grand up front," Carleton answered. "The same after the games are over."

"How did you cut the pole?" Frank asked.

"With the file," he said.

Joe nodded. "How did you get hold of Parrish's pole?"

"Before the trials, I hung around the stadium and made myself known so no one would think twice about seeing me in the locker room," Carleton said. "I stole one of the Americans' locker keys and had a copy made. I made the cut in Parrish's pole early Saturday morning before the trials began. To tell you the truth, I expected his pole to break sooner than it did."

Joe felt anger rising in his throat. Chuck Parrish could have been killed. And what about Vanessa? "Was it Jay Hamilton who met Vanessa at the hotel this morning?" he demanded. "He was the tall Neptunian?"

Carleton nodded. "Yeah. When I told him about you guys looking into the thing with Parrish, he set up the meeting. I gave him her E-mail address from my volunteers' phone book and lent him my costume."

"What did he plan to do with her?" Frank asked.

"He wasn't sure. Question her, see if you guys had found out anything, then decide what to do next. He really didn't expect y'all to follow."

"What about the astronaut shooting?" Officer Heiser asked. "You guys have anything to do with that?"

"No way," Carleton said. "Hamilton was just interested in messing up the pole-vaulting event."

Frank pointed to the starter pistol, which Officer Heiser held in his hand. "What about that? Did you guys have a few more surprises planned?"

"I lifted it from the officials' room," he said.

"With you guys poking into everything, things were getting tense. Hamilton wanted to be sure we could protect ourselves."

The officers handcuffed Carleton and put out an all-points bulletin for Jay Hamilton. Before they left, Detective Posten turned to Joe and Frank. "Let the authorities take it from here. You two have done a great job, but we don't want you getting involved in the attack on the astronaut. The CIA and the FBI are working on the case. Let them do their job."

The Hardys nodded, then said goodbye. "I don't think Carleton and Jay Hamilton had anything to do with the Cyrenian stuff, and neither do the cops," Frank said. "Which means there are some very dangerous guys—and maybe a girl—still running around out there."

Joe called the broadcast center and told Vanessa what had happened. She sounded relieved that Carleton was under arrest. Then she told Joe that the place was buzzing with gossip about all the crimes. The word was that Jay Hamilton and Carleton Fisher would be charged with everything.

"I'm not so sure about that," Joe told her. "It looks like we've solved only half of the crimes."

"I hope you'll let the government and the police take over now, Joe," said Vanessa.

"We'll see," was all Joe would say.

Tuesday morning the phone woke Frank at eight.

"Is this Mr. Hardy?" a thickly accented voice asked.

"Yes, this is Frank. Who's this?"

"This is Gregor Stefanov," the man said. "I am with the Ministry of State for the country of Gurnistan."

By now Joe was awake, too. "Yes, Mr. Stefanov," Frank said. Joe sat up when he heard Frank say the name. This was one of the guys Inda Radich had named!

"You met with a Miss Radich Sunday afternoon here on Stone Mountain."

"What makes you think that?" Frank asked.

"We have many agents on Miss Radich's trail."

"Really?" Frank said. "And why is that?"

"Miss Radich is a terrorist," the man said. "She is already responsible for many violent acts in our country. She came to the Olympics to continue her reign of terror against our people."

"That's not quite the way she tells it."

"I am confident of that, and that is why I have called. I am pleased to tell you that we have at last captured this dangerous terrorist. I personally arrested her this morning."

"Arrested her for what?" Frank asked.

"For the crossbow shooting of the Cyrenian astronaut during the opening ceremonies," the caller said. "She will be sent to Gurnistan to stand trial to answer for her terrorist acts."

"Why would she shoot the astronaut if he was her countryman?" Frank asked. Joe sat on the edge of his bed, trying to piece together the conversation even though he was hearing only half of it.

"She belongs to a radical faction determined to destroy the progress for peace that has been made between Cyrena and Gurnistan," the man said. "I'm sure she told you that Gurnistani assassins were behind the astronaut's attack."

Frank didn't say anything. He didn't want to let the man know anything more than he had to, at least until he knew which side to believe.

"Are you there, Mr. Hardy?" the man asked.

"Yes, I am," Frank answered. He picked up pencil and paper and started writing a note to Joe. "I saw a photograph of you, Mr. Stefanov, and it matched the description of the man I saw run down Coach Masily of the Cyrenian team."

"It was a heavy man, yes?" the caller said. "With dark hair and a beard?"

Again, Frank was silent.

"Please let me assure you that was not me," the caller said. "That was a picture of Miss Radich's henchman, name of Grigor Kissloff. We have also arrested him, as you will soon see."

"Excuse me?"

"I am hoping that you, your brother, and your friend from the broadcasting center will meet with me. I ask that you assist me in identifying the two criminals, Miss Radich as the woman driving away from the stadium after the astronaut was shot and her associate, Kissloff, as the hit-and-run driver."

Joe read the note that Frank was scrawling: "Stefanov is a gov agent, not the van driver. Radich was arrested—terrorist?"

"I had a feeling about her," Joe whispered.

"I would also like to take depositions from you regarding your conversation with Miss Radich," the caller continued.

"Where do you want to meet?" Frank asked.

"I have a suite at the Stone Mountain Conference Center," the man said. "We could have a stenographer take your deposition in our conference room. I urge you to assist me. Your testimony is vital."

"Just one moment, please," Frank said. He covered the receiver and told Joe what the man was asking.

Joe hesitated. The pole-vaulting event was due to start this morning, and he and Frank were due to help. But this was too important to miss.

"I say we go," Joe said finally. "It sounds legitimate—and if it's not, it might help us crack the case."

"We can be there by about ten o'clock, Mr. Stefanov," Frank said into the phone.

"Very good," the caller said. "I have reserved parking space ninety-eight at the conference center. Please make use of it. I am in the Granite Suite. I will see you there."

Frank hung up. "You know Detective Posten isn't going to like this. Maybe we shouldn't meet this guy."

"Come on, Frank," Joe said. "We can handle this. Besides, we'll let Detective Posten and Officer Heiser know where we're going. We'll leave a message."

The Hardys called Vanessa, then got ready to go. Before leaving the room, they left a message for Detective Posten and grabbed the brochure and map of Stone Mountain.

"What did you tell your supervisor?" Joe asked Vanessa when they met her outside her building.

"That I needed the morning off for personal business," Vanessa told him. "I'm going to try

135

to make up the hours later." She made a face at Joe. "I'm still not sure this is the best idea."

Joe shrugged. "It'll be fine."

As they headed out to Stone Mountain, Vanessa asked questions. "So who's telling the truth? Inda Radich or Gregor Stefanov?"

"My money's on Stefanov," Joe said. "I was right about Carleton, wasn't I?"

"I'm not sure who's lying," Frank admitted.

"We'll find out soon enough," Joe said. "You should be able to recognize this guy if he was the hit-and-run driver."

"Maybe not," Frank said. "He could be wearing a disguise. Or he could have been wearing a disguise that night."

"This could be a trap," Joe said. "We'd better be on our toes."

When they arrived at the conference center, Frank pulled the van slowly into the parking lot.

"There's spot number ninety-eight," Joe said as Frank drove by it.

"I think I'll park down here." Frank pulled the van into a spot in the far corner of the lot.

"Vanessa, why don't you go inside and hang around the reception area?" Frank said. "Joe, let's check out this reserved parking space. Maybe there was some reason we were asked to park there."

"I'd better go with Vanessa," Joe said. "We don't know what the deal is yet."

"Okay," Frank agreed. "I'll be there in a minute."

Frank watched Joe and Vanessa walk across the lawn and enter the building. He slipped out of the van and moved cautiously around the edge of the parking lot, making his way to number ninety-eight. When he got there, it was still empty.

Too late, he saw a movement in the hedge at the end of the parking space. Out stepped the man he had seen driving the hit-and-run van. The hot midmorning sun glinted off a small revolver clenched in his fist.

Chapter

15

"STEFANOV," Frank said.

"Yes, it is I, Mr. Hardy," the man said.

"You were lying about Inda Radich," Frank said.

"It wasn't all a lie," Stefanov said. "We do have her. It was not strictly an arrest, you understand. It is more a permanent detainment."

"Give up, Stefanov," Frank said. "The authorities know exactly where we are and why."

"Ah, but by the time they get here, I no longer will be."

Frank looked around. There wasn't another soul in the parking lot, and he didn't see any immediate escape route.

"Don't try to run away, my young friend,"

Stefanov said. "You would only bring on a premature end to this story. Now, let's join your brother and his lovely friend. Walk calmly toward the building. Remember, I will be right next to you."

"You can't pull this off, Stefanov. The conference center has to be full of people."

"And you think I wouldn't shoot you or any of them?" Stefanov laughed. "Why don't you put me to the test? It would be my pleasure to prove you wrong."

Frank obeyed. He knew enough about terrorism to realize that this guy wasn't lying. Terrorism was about making a point—and making it with violence.

Frank walked toward the building. His only chance was to signal Joe to clear out and call the authorities.

His plan was blown away a second later when Joe and Vanessa walked woodenly toward him. Close behind them was the other man whose photo Inda Radich had showed them the night before—Ivan Kalery. Frank felt as if he'd been punched in the stomach by a prizefighter. How were they ever going to get out of this one?

"All right, now let's all return to the parking lot for our ride," Stefanov said. "You must act natural, as if nothing's happening. If you give away your plight, you will be responsible for many deaths."

Vanessa caught her breath and was about to say something. Joe flashed her a warning look, and she swallowed her words, nodding slightly to him. She got the picture now.

The three captives were led to a long black car with tinted windows. Joe, Vanessa, and Kalery climbed into the back. Frank sat in the front next to Stefanov, who drove. Kalery kept his gun trained on Joe and Vanessa.

"So am I right, Stefanov?" Frank asked. "You were the one who drove the hit-and-run van, and the one who followed us into the tunnel after the astronaut was shot."

Stefanov nodded. "My associate and I were concealed at a distance when you and your brother used our ropes. We followed you and saw you talking to the authorities and then showing them our equipment."

"In all the chaos, no one noticed you, I'm sure," Frank said.

"With our stolen costumes, we had no trouble blending in," Stefanov admitted. "We stood only a few feet away while you talked to the authorities. Then we decided to advise you that you were in over your heads, as you Americans say. If that stupid guard had not seen me in the tunnel, our current expedition might not be necessary."

"Which one of you charming gentlemen gave me the kidney chop?" Joe asked from the back.

Stefanov smiled. "That would be my associate, Mr. Kalery. He followed you from your young friend's room, called in a purse-snatching report to clear the area of security, then delivered our message. It is a shame you chose to ignore it. We tried to warn you."

The car traveled away from the developed part of the resort, heading toward the campground.

"What about Vlad Kirov?" Joe asked. "Is he part of your gang?"

"Mr. Kirov has been useful at times, but he failed on a particularly sensitive project."

"You mean launching a rocket grenade into the archery center?" Joe remembered the incident at the bell tower.

"That is correct," Stefanov said. "Mr. Kirov has been permanently relieved of his duties and will no longer be participating in our activities."

Joe swallowed hard. If he'd read Stefanov right, Kirov had been harmed, maybe even assassinated.

"Where's Inda Radich?" Frank asked. "Did you plant the crossbow in her closet?"

"Yes, and she is safe for the time being," the Gurnistani said with a smile. "We have an interesting plan for her. Shall we say, she will soon be reaching her peak of fame." Stefanov let out a loud laugh, then pulled into a parking spot. He and Kalery yanked Vanessa and the Hardys out of the car.

The five hiked about a half-mile into the wilderness, then left the trail and cut through the woods to a boarded-up shack at the bottom of an abandoned granite quarry.

Kalery pulled a few loose boards off one window, then Stefanov ordered the Hardys and Vanessa to crawl inside. The Gurnistanis pushed their captives onto the floor, tied their hands behind them, bound their feet, and wound heavy duct tape over their mouths and around their heads.

"I'm not sure the gags are even necessary," Stefanov said. "No one could hear you screaming down here anyway. But we believe in taking precautions."

The Gurnistanis crawled out the window and boarded it back up. Frank, Joe, and Vanessa could barely hear their captors' footsteps as they left.

It was dark inside the shack. The boards on the windows and door let in only a few faint beams of light.

Frank scooted over to Joe and used his head to knock his brother onto his side.

"Hmph," Joe said from behind the duct

tape. But he knew what Frank had in mind. He felt Frank's fingers working at the ends of the duct tape on the back of his head.

After about ten minutes of concentrated work, Frank was able to peel the duct tape away from Joe's face and mouth. It came away with a loud ripping sound.

"Ouch," Joe said. "That stuff hurts."

Frank lay down with the back of his head near Joe's hands. Little by little, Joe managed to loosen the duct tape, then finally pull it away from Frank's head.

Joe moved to Vanessa and went to work on her gag in the same way.

"How long do you think they're going to keep us here?" Joe asked as he worked.

"My guess is forever," Frank said.

"That's encouraging," Vanessa mumbled as Joe peeled the tape from her mouth. "It's so dark in here."

"Let's see if we can let some light in." Joe said. "Follow me, Frank."

Frank scooted behind Joe until they both had reached the window.

"How's your shoulder-stand form?" Joe asked Frank. He rolled on his back to demonstrate. Rocking from side to side, he snaked his legs up the side of the wall.

Finally, he was practically upside down, his

legs and feet touching the window. Frank followed his lead.

"Okay, on the count of three, give it your best kick," he told Frank.

He and Joe pulled their legs out away from the window and held them there.

"One," Joe said. "Two . . . three!"

Together, they slammed their legs back into the window. Two sets of tied ankles crashed through the glass like a pair of sledgehammers, knocking down the plywood boards that had been nailed on the outside.

Frank and Joe rolled away from the window, over dozens of shards of glass. More pieces fell away from their bodies as they sat up.

With his hands still tied behind his back, Frank reached for a sliver that could serve as a knife, watched and guided his movements as he sat back-to-back with Joe, and cut away the ropes around his brother's wrists.

Finally, Joe was free. He quickly cut Frank's and Vanessa's ropes and knocked out the glass remaining in the window. Then the three of them escaped from the shack.

They quickly found the trail that led back to the campground.

"Where do you think they're holding Inda Radich?" Vanessa asked.

"I'm not sure," Frank said. "To tell you the

truth, I'm surprised she wasn't with us in the quarry shack."

"They might be holding her in their suite at the conference center," Joe said. "Wait a second. What did Stefanov say?"

"That Inda Radich would be reaching her peak of fame," Frank said. "Then he let out that creepy laugh."

Something suddenly clicked in Joe's mind. "Peak," he echoed softly. "The cable cars!" He'd read something about them in a tourist brochure. The large glass-enclosed cars took riders more than eight hundred feet up into the air for fantastic views at the summit of Stone Mountain. "There's a shuttle to the cable cars from the campground. This way," he said, taking a fork in the path and breaking into a half-run. Frank and Vanessa followed, and they reached the shuttle stop in minutes.

The shuttle was just pulling out. Frank flagged it down, and Joe turned to Vanessa. "Vanessa, take the other shuttle to the conference center. Call Detective Posten and Officer Heiser." He handed her the detective's business card. "Tell them it's an emergency."

"Be careful, Joe," she said.

"Okay. You watch yourself, too."

For Frank and Joe, it was a fifteen-minute shuttle ride to the Skylift. As they pulled up, Frank noticed Stefanov's car in the parking lot.

"Let's lay low for a while," Frank said. "They could be on their way to the top or still on the ground."

The Hardys looked up at a cable car that had begun its ascent up the mountain. The orange car was halfway up the side of the mountain, swaying gently on its pulley.

Another car was waiting for the next batch of tourists.

The Hardys saw about twenty people walking from the ticket taker to the cable car.

"Look." Frank nudged Joe. Stefanov and Kalery were in the middle of the crowd. "They're here!"

The Hardys ducked behind a truck. "Look who's with them," Joe said.

"That's what I was afraid of," Frank answered grimly. "Inda Radich."

Each of the two Gurnistanis gripped one of the Cyrenian's arms. Her lips were pursed tightly, and her dark eyes radiated fear.

"This is pretty bleak," Joe said. "What are we going to do?"

"Come on." Frank waited until the group of tourists passed. "We're going for a ride." The Hardys got in line and bought tickets. They entered through the turnstile and blended into the crowd, well behind Stefanov and Kalery. They managed to stay hidden as they stepped into the cable car.

With a lurch, the Skylift began its ascent. Frank and Joe squeezed through the crowd of passengers until they were directly behind the Gurnistanis.

"Now!" Frank whispered.

The Hardys shot into action. Frank grabbed Kalery, who was holding Inda Radich tightly. Joe slammed into Stefanov and grabbed his arms. The gun Stefanov had been holding under his jacket clattered to the floor. Terrified screams filled the air.

Before Kalery could make a move, Frank spun him around. He landed a crisp uppercut on his jaw. The Gurnistani dropped to his knees, then crumpled backward.

Inda Radich scooped up the gun, holding it on Kalery as Frank looked around the car for Joe. By now, most of the terrified passengers were flat on the floor or huddled in the corner. The employee who was manning the car stared wide-eyed at what was happening, not knowing what to do.

Suddenly, Stefanov bolted through the open window at the end of the car and hauled himself onto the glass roof. Joe flew after him.

The cable car rocked furiously as the two crawled across the roof.

Joe halted as Stefanov reached under his pants leg and pulled out a small pistol crossbow. He tried to get a quick bead on Joe, but the car was too unsteady. He hesitated, trying to take aim, and that's all Joe needed.

With one powerful lunge, Joe caught him. As they wrestled, Joe grabbed Stefanov's wrist and twisted it hard. Stefanov's grip relaxed, and the crossbow fell.

Stefanov rolled away from Joe, rocking the car violently.

Joe slid across the roof. Just as he was about to plunge over the side, his fingers caught the rim of the car. He gripped the metal tightly, dangling from the side of the car. By now, they were hundreds of feet above the ground.

Stefanov hadn't given up. He got to his feet and lurched over to Joe. Then he lifted one of his heavy boots to stomp on Joe's fingers.

Chapter

16

STEFANOV'S BIG BOOT hovered over Joe's right hand, then came crashing down. But the cable car was swaying so violently that the Gurnistani missed his target.

Joe's heart skipped a beat. The base of Stone Mountain was four hundred feet below. At this height, he'd never survive a fall.

In the car below, Frank was scrambling to pull himself through the open window at the end of the swaying car. Several of the other passengers helped boost Frank up.

With a sudden surge of strength, Joe hauled himself back up onto the roof. He lunged for Stefanov's ankle and sent him flying onto his back. As the huge man fell, he struck his head and was knocked out cold.

Joe dragged Stefanov back along the roof. With Frank's help, along with some of the passengers, they managed to wrestle Stefanov's bulk back inside the cable car and onto the floor.

"That was truly unbelievable," Joe said as he panted for air. He slumped, exhausted, next to Frank against the cable car wall. Inda Radich kept the Gurnistanis covered as the other passengers went on about what they had just witnessed.

When the cable car reached the top of the mountain, Vanessa was waiting for them, along with Officer Heiser and Detective Posten.

"How did you make it up here so fast?" Joe said in amazement.

"The police were in the conference center looking for us when I got there on the shuttle," Vanessa explained. "A park ranger brought us up on the maintenance road. It was a wild ride."

"We got your message and came right out," Detective Posten said, "but we couldn't locate you."

"Stefanov admitted to us that he drove the hit-and-run van," Frank said. "Also that Kalery was the guy who assaulted Joe."

"Stefanov just happens to be a crossbow

specialist," Joe said. "He told us they were the ones who shot the astronaut. Then they dumped the crossbow in Inda Radich's cabin."

"You pig." Inda Radich spat the words at Stefanov. "You may be under arrest here, but I will be sure you and your people pay for this in Cyrena and Gurnistan, too. Why can't you just stand up and fight like men instead of attacking innocent people thousands of miles from your homeland?"

"You have no proof of anything you say," Stefanov retorted. "I am an emissary of my country's government. I have diplomatic immunity. You cannot keep me against my will."

"Diplomatic immunity goes only so far," Detective Posten said. "We draw the line at multiple counts of attempted murder."

"You might want to check on Vlad Kirov, Officer, if you can find him," Frank said. "I'm afraid our suspects here may be charged with more than *attempted* murder."

Inda Radich turned to the Hardys and Vanessa. "They were going to kill me up here and dispose of my body in the wilderness," she said. "And after that, they had more terrorist activities planned. You saved many lives today. Thank you."

"Aw, shucks." Joe grinned. "It was a piece of cake."

Inda Radich shook her head. "I underestimated you Hardys, that's for sure."

"So did we," chimed in Detective Posten. "We actually thought those two would listen to us and let the authorities crack the case."

The two Gurnistanis were taken away in a police van, accompanied by Detective Posten, Officer Heiser, and several heavily armed officers in uniform. The ranger drove the Hardys, Vanessa, and Inda Radich back to the conference center. From there, they were escorted downtown by a police caravan.

Frank, Joe, Vanessa, and Inda Radich spent the next two hours giving their statements to the FBI. When they finished, Vanessa took off for the broadcast center. "Boy, do I have a scoop," she said. "I'll be the one to break the news."

The Hardys and Inda Radich left to find Terry and give him and his teammates the good news.

That evening the Cyrenians hosted an impromptu dinner in the party room at the Dead Heat. The U.S. pole-vaulting team had been invited, too.

"And now for our presentation," Terry said during the break between dinner and dessert. He had to tap his glass to quiet the noisy guests. "The U.S. pole-vaulting team has a special gift for the Hardys."

With the help of his coach and teammates, Chuck Parrish stood up. "We want to make Joe and Frank honorary team members," he said. Then he handed out the official U.S. Olympic Team's wardrobe—blazers, pants, warm-up suits, uniforms, and hats. As Frank and Joe took them, Chuck Parrish grinned. "Who knows? With Joe's skill as a vaulter, he may be on the team four years from now."

Joe smiled. "No, thanks. I'll leave that to the real competitors."

Applause filled the room, and Terry stood again. "Inda Radich and I also have a gift for the Hardy brothers, who have done a great service to our country." Terry turned to the Hardys. "We hope these small tokens will always remind you of the undying gratitude of the Cyrenian people for your courageous acts in our defense."

The brothers opened identical black velvet boxes and, with big smiles for the flashing cameras, held up the contents for all in the room to see: gold medals with ribbons of blue and gold stripes.

"The Cyrenian Order of Merit," Terry explained. "Medals of honor given to individuals who have faced great danger and outsmarted the enemy."

"Thank you all very much," Frank said as the applause finally died down. "When we came to the Olympics, the last thing we expected to receive was a gold medal."

"You Hardys are also honorary Cyrenian competitors," Terry said, gesturing to himself and the two bald runners on either side of him. "You have earned your place on our team."

"Thank you, Terry," Joe said. "We're very flattered." He nudged Frank. "We have just one question."

"Anything, Joe," Terry replied.

Joe tried to keep a straight face as he brushed back his blond hair. "Does this mean we have to shave our heads, too?"

Frank and Joe's next case:

The Hardys have come halfway around the world to experience one of the most spectacular and forbidding mountain ranges anywhere: the Himalayas. Their intention was to do some serious climbing, and they've gotten their wish . . . with one catch. Not only will they have to cope with the ice and snow and sudden drops, but they may also be heading straight into an ambush—set by a murderer! Two climbers were killed in a recent avalanche, and the leader of the expedition is convinced there was foul play. At the top of the list of suspects is Pasang, the uncle of Frank and Joe's friend. When Pasang suddenly vanishes without a trace, the boys realize that the stakes in their climb have just gone up. They're ascending a mountain of mystery, and their lives are on the ropes . . . in *Cliff-hanger,* Case #112 in The Hardy Boys Casefiles™.